An ANGEL in the FAMILY

a novel

Dan Yates

Covenant Communications, Inc.

OTHER BOOKS BY DAN YATES

Angels Don't Knock

Angels to the Rescue

Just Call Me An Angel

Published by Covenant Communications, Inc.
American Fork, Utah

Printed in the United States of America
First Printing: June 1998

05 04 03 02 01 00 99 98   10 9 8 7 6 5 4 3 2 1

ISBN 1-57734-282-8

PROLOGUE

Maggie took a lingering look around at the office where she had served as Gus' secretary for nearly a century now. This room had witnessed many wonderful events, but her work here would soon be reduced to the warm chambers of her memory. There was so much about the place she would miss, but the time for her final good-bye to it all was rapidly drawing near. She wished Gus could be here to lend a hand with some of the many things that had to be done before time ran out. Unfortunately, for her, Gus was in the middle of an orientation with the higher authorities in preparation for his part of what was to come.

On the desk, in front of her, lay the files of four individuals. There was a file for Samantha's brother Michael, one for Jenice Anderson, one for Brad Douglas, and of course—one for the good captain, himself. Each file represented an unresolved problem that the higher authorities had decreed had to be addressed before the big change could take place.

Maggie was glad that Gus had at least helped out with preparing the game plan before leaving for his orientation. However, the act of putting the plan into motion belonged solely to her now. This was to give her experience, the higher authorities had explained. Not that she didn't already have a degree of experience in matters similar to these. This time, however, the experience would come in an official capacity—not from simply lending a hand as a helpful secretary. The higher authorities were quick to point out the difference.

Maggie picked up the files for Michael and Jenice. "This is going to be the hardest," she said to herself. "Keeping Sam in the dark won't be easy, and her feelings about Jenice Anderson won't help much either." Maggie sighed as she remembered the first time Jenice's name had come to her attention. It was right here in this very office on the day Maggie and Samantha first met: the day Gus had caught Samantha in the elevator on her way to marry Bruce Vincent. Gus had brought Samantha to this office, where he tried to sell her on a revised contract for the original one he had botched with his typo. The contract that had linked Samantha's destiny with Jason Hackett's.

Samantha did sign a revised contract, but not before accepting Maggie's help to make some changes from the way Gus proposed it. One of those changes had been "the Bruce clause." Samantha had utterly refused to cross the line into a new dimension where she could be with Jason until Gus promised to find someone to take her place with Bruce. Gus had been given one year to get Bruce a wife. That was when Jenice's name came up. Maggie had efficiently extracted it from the computer as a possible candidate for Bruce's wife-to-be.

Bruce and Jenice met at Samantha's funeral, and some time later they became engaged. When Jenice began having second thoughts and wanted to call the whole thing off, Samantha became involved in her first angel assignment, and managed to get Bruce together with her best friend, Arline Wilson. The experience gave Samantha a deep dislike for Jenice Anderson, however, partly because Jenice was the sister of Rebecca Morgan, an obnoxious woman married to one of Bruce's friends, and partly because Samantha didn't like the way Jenice treated Bruce.

But—whatever the reason—the fact remained that Samantha didn't like Jenice Anderson. Now, Maggie was faced with the dilemma of bringing Samantha and Jenice together, face to face, again.

Laying the first two folders aside, Maggie picked up the one marked Brad Douglas. "Poor Brad," Maggie said. "If Gus had only paid more attention to business ten years ago, Brad's name wouldn't be on the delinquent list now. Oh well, what's done is done. With Sam and Jason's help, we'll just have to rectify that little mistake now, won't we?"

Maggie knew Brad's case would take longer than the others to rectify, but all the higher authorities required for now was a start on his case. Samantha and Jason could finish this one a little further down the road.

Maggie picked up the last folder, the one for the captain. She shook her head in mild disgust. "You shouldn't even be my problem, Captain," she said. "It was only through Gus' finagling that your name got thrown in with the others. Not that your case is any less important. But you will take some special handling. You're a tough one, all right." Maggie smiled as she contemplated an idea. "I think I'll just let Sam handle you, my friend. I'd say you've pretty well met your match in that one."

Maggie lay all the folders back on the desk and sat staring at them. "Where shall I start?" she asked. "A trip to George Glaser's office is definitely in order. I have a little item to drop off in Michael's mailbox, and then there's the problem of drawing Sam and Jason into the plan. That one has to be handled with extreme care. I'm sure I'll think of something."

Maggie figured the first thing in order should be one last review of the captain. She wanted to be sure all the details about him were fresh in her mind. "I certainly wouldn't want to botch the first assignment the higher authorities have ever entrusted to me personally," she smiled. Moving to her computer, she quickly set up a holographically enhanced playback of the event that had started it all with the salty old seaman. Leaning back in her chair, she drew in a deep breath and watched as it came into view in front of her.

* * *

Even now, with thrashing waves the size of mountains and winds howling like angry demons out of the blackness of the cold night sky, the sea held no fear for Captain Horatio Symington Blake. With a grip of steel, he clung to the wheel of the crude wooden vessel, fighting desperately to keep her bow turned into the face of the storm—a storm that lurked before him like the very jaws of death itself. What was there to worry about? he desperately tried to convince himself.

There had been other storms—hundreds of them over the years. And this crew could certainly be trusted. After all, they were hand picked, down to the last man. Never before had Blake taken such pains in picking a crew. But then, this was not just any voyage—not with the lady on board.

The man at the captain's side spoke nervously. "Aye, Capt'n, this be a bad one. The men and me, we be talkin', and not one man among us can remember ridin' out a storm like this here one. We be thinkin' Capt'n—well—we be thinkin' it be the lady. We think she be cursed."

It was first mate, Grayson—the one they called Curly—who had come up to the captain with a petition from the rest of the frightened crew.

"Cursed ye say?!" Blake shot back with a fire in his eye that always signaled he was not in a frame of mind to be trifled with. "Blast ye, man! How can ye say the lady be cursed? She be lying peaceful as sleep itself in her box, says I, just where we placed 'er before we set out to sea. There be no curse! This here storm be like any other ye've ridden out in yer miserable life, Curly. Get back to yer post, and tell the others ta do the same. Pay no heed to these howlin' winds, says I. In no time a'tol we'll be sailin' on seas smoother than the gold on the king's crown. Them be me words, matey."

Grayson swallowed hard and gathered his courage to speak his mind further. "No, Capt'n, ye be wrong. This here be no ordinary storm. This here storm be the keeper of the sea tellin' us we be carryin' a cursed cargo. The men and me, we put it to a vote, Capt'n. We want the lady thrown to the waves, coffin and all. It be the lady who goes to her icy grave, or it be us."

With the speed of lightning itself, Blake let go of the wheel, grabbing Grayson by the lapel of his shirt. "So, it be an icy grave ye want, Curly? Well then, an icy grave ye'll be havin'. But it be not the lady who goes into the waves—it be ye! I gave me word to deliver the lady over safe and sound to this here gentleman Oscar Welborn's family in the new world, I did. And, says I, all the storms that this here ocean can throw in my way won't stop me from keepin' me word. When Horatio Symington Blake gives his word, by the blazes, it be kept. And I'm givin' ye my word now, Curly, either ye get yer bones back to yer station or it's shark food ye'll become. What'll it be, matey?"

Soaked to the bone and shivering like a mouse in a cat's jaw, Grayson felt his courage drain away. "Ay, Capt'n," he meekly agreed. "I'll pass yer word on to the men. But by the stars, they'll not like one word of it. They have it in their heads the lady be cursed, and they be in fear of their very lives."

With an angry growl, Blake waved Grayson away and watched with contempt as the frightened first mate returned to the others. The loudness of the howling wind made it impossible for Blake to hear what was said between the men as Grayson approached them, one at a time. In his heart, the wise old captain knew trouble was a brewin'. Once these seagoing curs had it in their minds that the ship was cursed, there was nothing he nor any other clear-thinking man could do to dispel the thought.

Captain Blake was no stranger to trouble. He had spent his life on the sea and had dealt with every dispute man or nature could dream up. But—he had given his word. He had vowed to place the lady safely into the hands of Oscar Welborn's family. That's what he was paid to do, and by thunder, that's exactly what he planned to do. Nothing had ever kept Captain Horatio Symington Blake from keeping his word once he had given it. And nothing ever would. Not even death itself.

CHAPTER 1

Jason smiled at Samantha. He couldn't help thinking how beautiful she looked, silhouetted against the backdrop of the rolling pine-covered hills. From the time she was a child, she had loved these mountains. They were always her place of retreat when a problem came along, or sometimes she just used them for an escape from the everyday cares of the world. Even now, with the grandeur of unseen galaxies waiting to be explored, these mountains still called to her with enchanting magnetism.

"Looks like you were feeling homesick for your mountains," he said softly to his wife.

Samantha slid her arm through his and pulled him close to her. Closing her eyes, she drew in a deep breath of fresh, pine-scented mountain air. "You're right, I do get homesick for this place," she admitted. "But this time, my handsome little ghost, I had a special reason for wanting to come here. Do you remember the first time we were here, Jason?"

Jason laughed. "How could I ever forget? But actually it wasn't on this very spot. It was over there, next to the bend in that stream."

"It was not next to the stream, Jason," Samantha disagreed. "I remember it perfectly. I was standing right here when you appeared out of nowhere, and led me back to my granddad and the others who were searching for me."

"Sam," Jason said patiently, "you were five years old at the time. I'm telling you, it was by the stream. Come on, I'll show you the exact spot." Jason took Samantha's hand in his and started off in the direction of the stream. As they walked, he explained, "It was your birthday and you had a party at your grandfather's place just over the hill. Your dad brought you and a group of friends here on a nature walk. You spotted a squirrel and chased it into the woods. That's how you became separated from the others." Jason pointed to a spot near the stream just ahead. "Right there," he said. "That's where I found you. You were scared out of your wits."

"I admit I was scared," Samantha conceded, "but we were over *there* beneath that big pine, exactly where I remember seeing you, my cute little ghost."

Jason pulled Samantha to him and kissed her brow. "It happened right *here*, Sam. And you weren't the only one scared, you know. I've never told you my side of the story, have I?"

Samantha's eyes met Jason's. "No," she said. "You haven't. So tell me."

Jason sat down on a large flat rock near the stream. He pulled Samantha down next to him. "To put it in your words, Sam," he began. "I had only been a ghost a short time when Gus brought me here. You didn't know it, of course, but Gus is the one who put that squirrel in your path. He wanted to lure you away from the others, and he knew you well enough to know the squirrel would do the trick."

"What?" Samantha blurted out. "Gus planned it that way? He deliberately led a five-year-old girl into these woods and let her get lost? Just wait till I see HIM again."

"Take it easy, Sam. Gus had his reasons."

"Ha! Gus always has his reasons, but none of them make any sense. And what about you, Jason Hackett? You just stood by and watched while he did such a thing?"

"Come on, Sam. You know me better than that. I didn't know what Gus was up to until after the fact."

Samantha was still stewing. "So what was his excuse, Jason? Let me guess, he just has a thing about ruining a five-year-old's birthday, right?"

"No, Sam, he didn't get you lost to ruin your birthday. He got you lost because he knew when I saw you so scared, my heart would long for the woman you would someday become. He was right, too. Appearing to you and leading you back to safety was my idea, not his. At least that's what I thought until he later spilled the beans that the whole thing was his plan. You see, up until that time I had no idea I was any different from any one else who had died. I never dreamed I was slated to stay on this side for the next twenty years. Not until Gus broke the news to me about his typo, and explained the contract securing my destiny to yours. If I'd never had such a deep experience with you before he sprang the whole thing on me, I probably would have told him where to get off. Much as I hate to admit it, Gus knew what he was doing."

"So what you're saying is, Gus got me lost to soften you up for spending the next twenty years playing ghost?"

"In a nutshell, Sam. And it worked."

Samantha thought for a moment. "I guess getting lost in the woods was worth you hanging around 'til I grew up. If that's what it took."

"That's what it took, Sam."

"Okay, explain something else to me," Samantha said, taking the subject one step further. "Why did I see you in the woods, and then not see you again for twenty something years after that? The rules state that once a person sees an angel, the angel can never be invisible to them again. So, why didn't it happen when I saw you in the woods?"

Jason shook his head. "I only know what Gus told me. He said the rule only works when the angel is seen through the eyes of an adult. Just because a little girl sees an angel once, doesn't mean she'll see the angel again, even if the angel happens to be close to her. Don't ask me to explain it. Ask Gus the next time you see him."

Samantha shrugged. "Okay, I will."

Samantha rolled over on her back and stared upward through the swaying branches at the azure blue sky beyond. Suddenly, something caught her eye. "Look at that, Jason," she said excitedly, pointing to the sky. "Those clouds are forming a sentence. Have you ever seen anything like it?"

Jason glanced up. "Well I'll be darned," he laughed. "You're right. And no, I haven't."

The clouds were spelling out the words *What if . . . .* It was almost as if a skywriter in an airplane had put them there.

"What do you think, Jason?" Samantha asked excitedly. "Is someone trying to tell us something, or what?"

"Tell us something? What are you talking about, Sam? They're just clouds."

"They might be just clouds, but clouds don't spell out sentences. Someone is trying to give us a message. Maybe it's the higher authorities."

"Nah," Jason said, still looking at the clouds. "Just a coincidence. Look, they're already blowing away."

"I don't think so," Samantha argued. "Clouds don't spell out words. Someone is trying to tell us something. What if—what if we're supposed to ask ourselves, 'What if . . .'?"

Jason laughed. "That's the craziest thing I've ever heard, Samantha Hackett."

"It's not crazy, Jason. Think about it. Why else would we both see a question written in the clouds? We're supposed to ask ourselves, *What if?* I just know it."

"What if what?" Jason asked, throwing up both hands. "It was just a coincidence, Sam. Nothing more."

"I know!" Samantha exclaimed, her face lighting up with excitement. "We're supposed to ask ourselves what if Gus had never made the typo. What would have happened to us then? Where would we be now?"

"Sam, let it go," Jason pleaded. "Thinking about what might have been can only lead to trouble. The important thing is, it all worked out and we're together now."

"Jason, sometimes I don't know what to think about you. You can be just plain boring at times. Get with it—this is exciting!"

"Okay, I give up. I'll play your little 'what if' game. What if we drop this whole subject and get back to something more logical?"

Samantha paid no attention to Jason's logical nonsense. She was having far too much fun with her version of the 'what if' game. "What if the typo had never have happened?" she continued. "That would mean you and I would have lived our lives at the same time. Ooh, this gives me goose bumps, just thinking about it. How do you suppose we would have met, Jason?"

Jason shook his head, perplexed. "I don't know how we would have met. What possible difference does it make? It didn't happen that way, so why worry about it?"

Samantha gave her husband a poke in the arm. "Come on, Jason. Think of some ways we could have met. Do you suppose it might have been in college? Who knows, you might have been my English professor or something."

Now Samantha had Jason's attention. "English professor," he grimaced. "No, Sam. I'd have been a chef, a darn good one. I'd probably have owned my own terrific restaurant on the exclusive side of town. Maybe even a chain of restaurants. But an English professor? Not hardly. That's the most ridiculous idea I've heard you come up with yet."

"You can't just assume you'd have been a chef," Samantha reasoned. "For all you know, you might never have learned to cook at all. And what's so ridiculous about your being an English professor? After all, you are somewhat of a poet, aren't you?"

"Me? A poet? Where did you ever get an idea like that?"

"At the movie theater, remember? The day I went to the show with Arline. You were there the whole movie, embarrassing the life out of me."

"Oh yeah, I remember," Jason said with a grin. "Arline had no idea I was there, so she couldn't figure why you kept laughing. You finally got up and ran out of the theater. Now that, my little Samantha, was what I call a fun game. Beats the heck out of this 'what if' stuff."

"Yeah, well, be that as it may, that's when you quoted your poem to me. Something about a handicapped fly."

"The one-eyed fly?" Jason laughed. "You still remember that?"

"How could I forget? That was the worst poem I ever heard. But it was a poem, and it proves you do have some talent. Not much talent maybe, but as much as any of the English professors I had in college. Talk about boring. Those guys could talk a person to sleep in the middle of a drummer's convention."

"Uh huh. You find English professors boring, and you equate me with them. Thanks, Sam. I needed that."

"Oops, sorry about that. I put my foot in that one, didn't I? I admit, you can be boring at times, but not like those guys. Forgive me?" she smiled.

"It'll cost you a kiss."

Samantha kissed him. "Umm," she said. "I might have to call you boring more often if it gets me that kind of punishment. Now come on, get with it. You come up with a way we might have met."

Jason shrugged. "I don't know how we would have met. What difference does it make? Gus did make the typo, I did court you as an angel, and we are together now. Forget it, okay?"

"I won't forget it," she insisted. "I think someone arranged those clouds to put this question in our minds. I'm going to ask Maggie. She'll know. Her computer has the answer to any question in the universe."

Jason frowned. "I don't know, Sam. Some things are best left alone, and I think this is one of them."

"Hogwash, as my Uncle Mac would say. This is something I want to know, and I'm not dropping it."

"Sam, I . . ."

"Tut, tut, tut, my cute little ghost," Samantha said, taking Jason by the hand and standing abruptly. "Come on. Let's pay Maggie a visit."

Jason gave in, and since angels have a way of traveling long distances in a very short time the two of them were just outside Gus' office in two ticks of the clock. Jason opened the door for her, as was his habit, and Samantha stepped inside. "Wow!" she exclaimed at what she saw. "You're redoing the office, Maggie. It looks great, but how did you ever get Gus to approve this?"

Maggie was standing on a step stool hanging a recently painted celestial version of a Norman Rockwell on the wall. "Ha," she laughed. "Gus didn't get any say in the matter. The higher authorities approved it. What do you think, Sam? Does the picture look good here, or would it be better over my desk?"

"The higher authorities approved it?" Samantha asked, somewhat surprised. "I didn't know they ever got involved in things like this, Maggie? What's the occasion?"

"They just wanted the office brightened up," Maggie said, letting it go at that even though Sam had the impression she wanted to say more. "What about the picture, Sam?"

Samantha studied the picture closely. She had always loved Norman Rockwell's work. Here on this side of forever it was even more enthralling, mainly due to the brilliant celestial coloring and three-dimensional layout. This painting depicted a young teenage driver at the wheel of his father's car with a wide-eyed guardian angel staring nervously at the road ahead. The perfect picture for an office that dealt with the mortal world on an everyday basis.

Samantha gave a nod of approval. "Leave it right there, Maggie. It's perfect."

Then, looking around the room, something else caught her interest. "Oh, Maggie," she exclaimed. "I love what you've done with Gus' desk. Cherry wood is my favorite, and it's so much bigger than his old relic. Where did he get that thing anyway, from some government overstock auction down below?"

"I have no idea where he got it," Maggie laughed. "It was here the day I started. What do you think of the leather chair I picked to go with the desk?"

Samantha slipped into the chair. "Wow! What would it be like? If I could have a setup like this at the school where I sub, I'd want to spend every day in class. This is pure luxury."

"I thought you'd like it," Maggie grinned. "In fact, I picked it with your taste in mind."

"You did?" Samantha asked. "Why?"

"Let's just say I know you have good taste," Maggie responded.

Samantha ran her hand over the smooth surface of the desk. "So what did you do with Gus' piles of clutter?"

"That's what all these new filing cabinets are for, Sam. Everything's filed away where it belongs for once."

"You took it on yourself to clean Gus' desk?" Samantha grimaced. "I don't want to be here when he finds out."

"He already knows," Maggie explained. "The higher authorities again."

"The higher authorities had you clean up Gus' desk? Now there's a hot one. What did you do, hire a front-end loader to come in and haul it away?"

"I should have hired one," Maggie agreed. "You can't believe the things I found in that pile of rubble he called a filing system. Outdated interstellar memos, old grocery lists for things he was supposed to pick up on his way home—there was even a thank-you note from your Grandfather Collens. It was still there from the time Gus let him visit when you were a mortal schoolteacher."

"You're kidding, Maggie. That was over a year ago. But, knowing Gus, I shouldn't be surprised."

"Speaking of Gus," Jason cut in. "Where is the guy, anyway?"

Maggie seemed a little taken back by the question. "Gus?" she said, stepping back off the stool. "Where is Gus? Uh—let's see, he's in a meeting with the higher authorities, I think."

"You think?" Jason asked.

"Gus doesn't tell me every little thing he's up to," Maggie excused herself. "I'm sure that's where he is, though. He did mention something about a meeting with them."

Samantha noticed a small box of things on the floor next to Gus' new desk. Right on top was a picture of a very neat-appearing woman. Samantha picked up the picture. "Is this Gus' wife?" she asked.

"Yes, Sam. That's Joan," Maggie answered. "The box you found it in contains some of Gus' personal items I removed from the desk when I cleaned it."

"Joan, huh," Samantha remarked. "She's beautiful, Maggie. What's she like?"

Maggie walked over to where Samantha was seated and took the picture from her. "Joan is a wonderful lady, Sam. Gus is a lucky man to share a contract with her. Wanna hear how they got together? It's a neat story."

"Yeah," Samantha smiled. "I do want to hear it."

Maggie grinned and started her explanation with a question. "You're a schoolteacher, Sam. Do you remember reading about a Joan in the history books?"

"You don't mean Joan of Arc?" she asked.

Maggie nodded.

Samantha took the picture back from Maggie and studied it closely. "No way, Maggie. This woman is too beautiful and too fragile to be Joan of Arc."

"Well, you're right, Sam. This Joan is not *the* Joan of Arc from history, although they did live at the same time and in the same city. At least, when they were both young girls—which has a lot to do with how Gus met Joan. Tell me, Sam, what do you remember about Joan of Arc?"

Samantha thought a moment. "Joan of Arc? Well, let's see. She lived in the early fifteenth century, she was born in France of peasant parentage, and she claimed to hear voices and see visions from the time she was thirteen. She led the French armies against the English and beat the pants off them. That's about all I remember, Maggie."

"You did very well, Sam. Taking her story a step further, it was her efforts that united the French people under the leadership of King Charles VII, and put an end to the English dreams of dominance over France. Joan was later captured by the English, and subsequently put to death."

"Okay," Samantha said. "So what does a woman thinking she heard voices have to do with Gus?"

"You're not giving the woman credit, Sam. She *did* hear the voices and *see* the visions. And guess who was in charge of providing her with those visions?"

"Maggie," Samantha said. "You're not telling me that Gus . . ."

"I'm telling you it really was Joan's mission to save France at the time. She was contracted for the job, and Gus was in charge of her contract. Back then, Gus was an angel, like you and Jason are now. The Special Conditions Coordinator at the time gave Gus the assignment. You know Gus, he couldn't get the job done without creating some sort of trouble. He managed to get to France all right and even found the right city—it was called Domremy back then. That's when his problem began. He looked up a thirteen-year-old girl named Joan, and wasted no time in making an appearance."

Samantha broke out laughing. "Gus appeared to the wrong girl?"

"The real Joan of Arc lived on the other side of town," Maggie chuckled. "By the time Gus figured out his mistake, it was too late. He had pinpointed the wrong Joan as the one mortal who could see and hear him."

"Now wait a minute, Maggie," Samantha interrupted. "Isn't there something about a child not being subject to that rule? Like when I saw Jason in the woods on my fifth birthday?"

"You were five," Maggie explained. "The cut-off age for that particular rule is eight. Joan was well beyond that point when she saw Gus, and she was stuck with him. So, she agreed to become his go-between. Gus made holographical recordings, which this Joan in turn played for the real Joan of Arc. Of course she always managed to stay out of sight when playing the recording, so the real Joan of Arc was never the wiser. And I'm sure you can guess what happened to Gus when his Joan added a few years, can't you?"

"The same thing that happened to Jason as he watched me grow up?"

Now it was Jason's turn to interrupt. "Are you saying Gus did his courting as an angel, like I did with Sam?"

"Almost like you, Jason. Except Gus didn't have a Bruce to compete with. That and the fact that Gus was a little slower than you. It took Gus another century after Joan joined him on this side before he could gather the nerve to propose to her."

"I can't believe it," Samantha grinned. "Gus has a romantic side. Don't that beat all?"

Jason put a hand to his head. "Gus? Romantic?" he said. "Ha! Tarzan was more romantic than Gus. Joan has my condolences. All I have to say is it's a good thing the French army didn't have to depend on Gus to type up their travel orders. They probably would have ended up looking for the English army somewhere around the Red Sea."

"Not nice, Jason," Maggie mildly rebuked.

Samantha's rebuke came a little stronger. "Jason Hackett," she scolded. "You should be ashamed of yourself! I think it's a wonderful story. You can plan on having Gus and Joan over for dinner in the very near future, and you can just plan the fanciest French spread your little chef's head can contrive."

"All right, Sam, I'll do the dinner bit. But if you plan on crying all night over how romantic the two of them are together, you can furnish your own box of Kleenex."

Samantha scowled at Jason as she returned the picture of Joan to the box on the floor. "I've never met your husband either, Maggie," she said. "Is Alvin on a famous page in history, too?"

A warm glow appeared in Maggie's smile. "No," she explained. "Alvin never made the history books. Our lives were more like yours and Jason's would have been without Gus' typo. We spent our time in mortality together when the world was a little younger. Our families sailed from England to the new world on the same ship. Alvin and I were part of the first group to settle in the New England colonies. When you fix that special dinner, Jason, why don't you just add a couple more plates. That way, the two of you can meet my Alvin the same time you meet Joan."

"You got it, Maggie," Jason smiled. "It's the least I can do after all you and your computer have done for Sam and me. Speaking of which, your computer is the reason we dropped in. My nosy little wife has a question she thinks it can answer."

Maggie looked back to Samantha. "You have a question, Sam? So—let's have it. What's on your mind?"

"I'm sorry, Maggie," Samantha apologized, still scowling at Jason. "My insensitive husband makes it sound like your computer is the only reason we ever come here to see you. I do have a question, though. I was just wondering, if Jason had lived when he was supposed to, how would the two of us have met? Can your computer tell us the answer to that one?"

A strange smile appeared on Maggie's face. "Good question, Sam," she agreed. "Let's pull up your file and see what happens."

Samantha watched as Maggie stepped to her desk and keyed in a command on her computer. A second later Samantha's personal file appeared on the screen, or so it seemed at first look. Maggie's trained eye apparently caught a problem.

"This is strange," Maggie observed thoughtfully. "Your file seems to be locked."

"Locked?" Samantha asked. "What does that mean?"

"It means I can't open your file. At least not all the way. It appears to allow only limited access."

"I don't get it, Maggie. I thought your computer never broke down."

"It's not broken down, Sam. Someone with higher access than me has your file locked. I can input your question, but I'm not sure how much good it will do with the limited access we have at the moment."

"How about Jason's file? Is there a chance you can get into his?"

Maggie shook her head. "Since you and Jason are sealed by a contract, you no longer have separate files. Your records are joined in this one single file."

Samantha looked at the screen and did her best to figure out what was going on. "You said you could try my question, Maggie. Go ahead and see what happens."

"All right, Sam, I'll give it a try." Maggie typed in the question and waited to see if an answer came up. It did. A message appeared on the screen, which Maggie read aloud.

"ASSUMING DESTINY HAD TAKEN ITS DESIGNED COURSE, SAMANTHA AND JASON WOULD HAVE MET WHEN THEY WERE INTRODUCED BY SAMANTHA'S BROTHER, MICHAEL."

"All right!" Samantha exclaimed. "Michael would have introduced us. Good old Michael. I set him up with enough dates in our time, it's only fitting he would have returned the favor by introducing me to my future husband. Ask your computer how Michael and Jason would have met."

Maggie nodded and typed in this question. Again the answer appeared on the screen. This time, however, Samantha wasn't quite as excited.

MICHAEL WOULD HAVE MET JASON WHEN JASON SAVED HIS LIFE.

"Saved my brother's life?" Samantha gasped. "How? When? Ask your computer to tell us more, Maggie. Will Michael be all right even though Jason can't be there as destiny had planned?"

Maggie quickly entered her question. Once more the answer appeared on the screen.

WITHOUT JASON THERE, MICHAEL WILL LOSE HIS LIFE. JASON IS THE ONLY ONE APPROVED.

"No!" Samantha shouted. "This can't be! Please, Maggie, ask your computer what we can do. There must be something."

One more question entered brought yet another answer to the screen.

THE TIME OF MICHAEL'S DANGER IS NEAR. JASON IS THE ONLY ONE APPROVED TO SAVE MICHAEL'S LIFE. HE MAY DO IT AS AN ANGEL, BUT HE MUST HAVE THE HELP OF A MORTAL. TIME IS OF THE ESSENCE. IT IS SUGGESTED YOU MOVE QUICKLY.

Samantha blinked her eyes then read the screen again. It didn't change. "Maggie," she pleaded. "Isn't there something you can do to get more information out of the computer? My brother's life is at stake here."

"I'm sorry, Sam. Your file is locked, and I can't get any more information. I can set Jason up to work with a mortal, but we have to be careful who we choose. It'll have to be someone who will accept Jason quickly. We don't have much time to prove his angelic qualities to a doubter right now."

Samantha paced the floor nervously. "There's only one person for Jason to work with," she said. "And that's Michael himself. It's only logical."

"Can't do it, Sam. Michael and Jason are brothers-in-law. They're too close; it's against the rules."

"What do you mean against the rules, Maggie? Gus approved me to work with my Uncle Mac when my cousins Lisa and Julie were in trouble. Why can't you approve brothers-in-law? They're not as close as niece and uncle."

"You said it yourself, Sam. Gus approved it. Gus has more authority than I have. I can approve one mortal for Jason to work with, but it can't be anyone as close as Michael."

Jason spoke up. "Arline Wilson," he said. "Arline has seen me. We won't have to waste time in proving who I am to her."

Maggie shook her head. "You both know that Bruce and Arline are on their honeymoon in Hawaii. Michael, on the other hand, will soon be boarding a cruise liner in the Caribbean Sea."

"Michael is where?" Samantha shouted. "How do you know that, Maggie?"

Maggie appeared a little shaken at Samantha's direct question. "I—uh—happened to see it in my computer before it locked up. I also noticed that Jenice Anderson is taking the same cruise liner."

"Jenice Anderson?" Samantha nearly fainted at hearing Maggie mention her name. "Jenice and my brother are on a cruise ship together?"

"Now take it easy, Sam," Maggie soothed. "Your brother's life is in danger here, remember? There's a good chance Jenice Anderson can help."

"NO WAY!" Samantha shouted. "Maggie, I don't want that woman anywhere near my brother. And if you're thinking of using *her* as Jason's counterpart, FORGET IT!"

Maggie waited patiently until Samantha had finished speaking. When she spoke, her voice was calm. "Sam, Jenice is the logical person to use for Jason's go-between to mortality. It shouldn't take long at all to convince her he's really an angel."

Samantha wasn't having any of it. "That's absurd, Maggie. What makes you think Jenice Anderson would accept Jason. She's never seen an angel before."

"Think about it, Sam," Maggie said persuasively. "Jenice never actually saw you or Jason, but she was there on Howard Placard's beach when Arline was talking with you. The day Bruce parachuted to the beach, you remember."

"Sure I remember, Maggie, but—"

Maggie held up both her hands. "But nothing, Sam. The time at Howard's beach just might be enough to give Jason a head start in proving himself to her. Especially if I toss in a little visual aid."

"Visual aid?" Samantha asked, still in shock at the thought of Jenice Anderson being involved with her brother.

"Yeah," Maggie continued. "Visual aid. A Selected Event Shown by Holographically Enhanced Regeneration. You know, you used a few of them when you were working with your Uncle Mac. In fact, they were quite effective, as I recall."

CHAPTER 2

Jenice Anderson stared at the burly man sitting across the cluttered desk from where she was standing. It wasn't that she opposed what he had said; it was just that she wasn't sure she heard him right. This was George Glaser, the most tight-fisted man with a dollar of any newspaper editor in the country. Everyone knew that.

"You want to send me to cover a story on a cruise ship?" she repeated his words suspiciously. "To the Caribbean? This has to be some sort of joke. There's no way you'd send this reporter on an assignment to the Caribbean unless there was something in it for you. 'Fess up, there's a catch here somewhere. What is it, George?"

George spit the big wad of gum he had been chewing into the metal trash can next to his desk. It landed with a loud thud. Wiping his mouth with the back of his stout, hairy hand, he glared at Jenice. Jenice hated his chewing gum habit. She thought it was disgusting the way he would add stick after stick to the wad in his mouth until it became so large it would barely fit, then he'd spit it out and start all over again with a fresh stick.

"What's the big deal, Anderson?" he growled in a deep gravely voice. "I got a hot tip there's a story here."

Opening his center desk drawer, he removed one of two legal-size envelopes and tossed it to her. "The boat leaves in just over three hours," he sneered. "I want you on it, Anderson. The envelope contains your ticket and enough dough to cover all expenses for the next couple of weeks."

Jenice checked the unsealed envelope. George was telling the truth. The ticket was there, as well as a substantial amount of cash, mostly in hundred-dollar bills. Her mind whirled in confusion and disbelief. In the three and a half years she had been reporting for the *Morning Municipal,* she had never seen George Glaser do anything to match this. "What sort of story am I looking for?" she asked dubiously.

George raised both hands in an exaggerated shrug. "Hey, my tipster didn't say. Just keep your eyes open, Anderson. You're a reporter. You'll know a story when it pops up."

Jenice was more skeptical than ever. "You're sending me on a cruise ship through the Panama Canal and into the Caribbean Sea chasing after some story, and you're not even sure what the story is? And to top it all off, you're paying for the whole thing? It just doesn't add up. There's something you're not telling me. What is it?"

Fire blazed in George's eyes. "Jenice, I want you on that boat, and if you don't leave now, you won't have time to do your packing. Now get out of my office. I have a newspaper to run."

Jenice shook her head and shoved the envelope into her purse. "Okay, George, if that's what you want. Who am I to look a gift horse in the mouth? I assume you want me to stay in touch."

"Yeah—yeah—yeah—stay in touch," he mumbled. "Just get going, will you? And close the door on your way out."

As Jenice stepped through the door into the outer office, she ran into fellow reporter Bob Draper. Bob was obviously waiting for her. The walls on George's office were just thick enough to keep a conversation from being understood, but not thick enough to hide George's booming voice. Especially when he yelled, which was most of the time.

"What's the old boy all shook up about this time?" Bob asked, as soon as he was sure Jenice had the door closed. "You're not fired, or anything, are you?"

"Fired?" Jenice laughed. "Not hardly. Why would George fire his number one reporter? He's sending me after a hot story, Bob. I'm going on an all-expenses-paid cruise to the Caribbean. Eat your heart out, pal."

Bob's chin dropped. "You're going where?" he gasped.

"You heard me," Jenice teased. "I'm after a story so big even George is forced to put up the cash to pay my way."

Bob was overwhelmed. "George is actually sending you after a story on a Caribbean cruise liner. Are you serious?"

"Of course I'm serious, why wouldn't I be? I am the logical one to go after the big stories, don't you agree?"

The spark in Bob's eyes indicated a jealousy that went beyond mere professional rivalry. "You will behave yourself, won't you, darling? After all, we are practically engaged, and there's bound to be lots of single men on the cruise."

Jenice had already started to walk away, when she stopped in midstride. "We're what?" She stared at him. "Bob, we've dated a couple of times but that's it. Where did you ever get the idea we're practically engaged?" She shook her head and added lightly, "Besides, I'm just not a marrying kind of girl. You should know that."

Bob stepped toward her and took her hand. "I know you're afraid of commitment," he said earnestly, "but I keep hoping you'll have a change of heart. I am crazy about you, you know."

Jenice sighed. "Look, Bob, it's not that I have anything against you personally. You're a great guy. It's just that—"

"Yeah, I know," Bob interrupted. "You don't need a husband to anchor you down whenever you get a chance to chase after one of your dreams. Like this Caribbean cruise," he added dejectedly.

Jenice gently extricated her hand from Bob's. "I know it's hard for you to understand, but the sort of adventure I crave goes far beyond cruising on a crowded ship or visiting a few tourist traps. I want to explore places where few, if any, others have ever been. I dream of climbing Mount Everest, or going on an African safari. Some day I'd like to learn to scuba dive so I can explore the bottom of the ocean. These are the kinds of adventure I crave. And yes, having a husband would get in the way of my dreams. Not that I don't think marriage is good. That is, if two people are deeply enough in love with each other." Jenice smiled, and pinched Bob playfully on his cheek. "You and I can always be good friends," she said. "But let's let it go at that, okay?"

"But I love adventure, too," Bob persisted. "I can do the things you describe, Jenice. Just give me the chance to prove it."

Jenice took a breath, remembering that she had heard this same argument before from her old fiancé, Bruce Vincent. Only in Bruce's case, he came through with flying colors. He actually did prove himself to be an adventuresome sort by skydiving from a plane onto

Howard Placard's private beach. Jenice had suggested the stunt as a way of convincing Bruce that the two of them weren't compatible enough for marriage. Of course, she had had absolutely no idea he'd actually go through with it. Thank goodness Bruce had fallen in love with Arline Wilson by the time he made the jump. Now he and Arline were very happily married.

There had been one man, however, who had come very close to breaking through Jenice's wall of defense, but that was all in the past now. Her decision on that rainy day in Paris had put an end to any hope of ever reviving that one. All that she had left were the memories, and what memories they were. Unfortunately, the trouble with good memories is that they're so often accompanied by a measure of pain. Which was why she kept those memories pushed as far to the back of her mind and heart as possible. And this moment was no exception. She forced her thoughts back to the present and to Bob.

"You're a good reporter," she said earnestly, looking him straight in the eye. "It's what you love and what will bring you happiness. Admit it, that's *your* dream, and one of these days you'll meet that special woman who can share your dream with you. Until then, you and I can always take in a movie or have dinner together once in a while. Okay?"

She leaned forward and kissed Bob on the cheek. Then, without giving him a chance for any further argument, she slipped out the door on her way to get packed.

* * *

As the door closed behind Jenice, George Glaser shoved a fresh stick of gum in his mouth, adding it to the wad already there. As he took a second envelope from his desk drawer, an evil grin crossed his face. Slowly he thumbed through the stack of green bills inside.

I have no idea who the lady was that gave me this bribe, he mused. *But who cares? She offered me ten G's to send a female reporter on a two-week cruise to the Caribbean, which she also paid for. Well, my mother didn't raise no dummies. I'll laugh all the way to the bank, and Miss Jenice Anderson will have a lovely two-week vacation. I might even consider giving her a small bonus when she gets back. Say—fifty bucks. Nah. I'll keep the dough for myself. She can have the trip.*

CHAPTER 3

Michael Allen leaned against the ship's railing and stared list-lessly out across the vast, calm Caribbean Sea. The salty smell and the feel of a cool, misty breeze against his face teased his senses with a sensual calmness that matched perfectly the melancholy of his mood. Here, on the forward deck of the luxury liner, *The Wandering Star,* reminiscing came easy. There were so many memories. Like those of a young boy at his Grandfather Collens' ranch in the moun-tains near Payson, Arizona. How he loved exploring the rugged woods and spectacular canyons in the mountains surrounding the ranch. It was those times, at the ranch, that nourished his early yearnings for wanderlust that would only gain momentum as he grew into a man. These memories came as sweet as a bowl of fresh strawberries picked from his Grandmother Collens' cherished garden and served with a generous portion of sugar, cream, and her special brand of love.

Some memories weren't so sweet. Like the rainy afternoon, next to the Eiffel Tower, where he waited in vain for *her* to join him—as she had promised to do. Or like losing his beloved sister in a freak elevator accident, and of all things missing her funeral. These were the two most tragic events of Michael's life, and the irony of it all was how the two were related.

After leaving his heart in Paris, Michael dealt with the pain just like he dealt with any problem. He threw himself smack in the middle of an adventure. In this case, he signed on as a kitchen aid on a cargo ship bound for China. Like always, he didn't bother leaving a forwarding address. By the time his family found him, Samantha had been gone more than two months. That's when he returned home and found a job, with the idea of changing his lifestyle once and for all.

Michael had no idea how he had won tickets for this Caribbean cruise. He couldn't even remember entering the contest. One thing for sure, it couldn't have come at a better time. With the exception of weekends, and a couple of holidays, Michael had been glued to his job every day for the past year. Not that there was anything wrong with being a security guard for the local museum; it was an okay job as nine-to-five jobs go. But it was like hanging an anchor around his neck, and he desperately needed to get away. Anywhere would do. Then, the tickets showed up in his mail box one morning—and here he was.

Not once in the past year had he considered returning to his first love, which was painting. Picking up a brush always brought a rush of memories. Memories of Paris, and of *her*. The last canvas he had painted, in fact, was a scene of the Eiffel Tower with *her* in the fore-ground. Selling this picture, as he had done with the others, was out of the question. Instead, he donated it to the museum the day he went to work there. The museum was grateful to get it, and displayed it in a front window where it could be enjoyed by anyone passing by. The only problem Michael had with this arrangement was that it meant passing by it every day on his way to and from work. Seeing her radiant smile certainly didn't help the forgetting process.

The sun was just beginning to set over the Caribbean, sending brilliant orange streamers up through cotton candy clouds lying thick on the edge of the summer sky. Off to the west, the tiny island of Vieques lay silhouetted against a backdrop of the vast Atlantic. It was breathtaking.

Shoving both hands in his pockets, Michael turned his back to the wind. From the far end of the ship came the first sounds of the band warming up for the evening festivities of dancing and dining. Michael would stay clear of this part of the cruise. All interest in things such as dancing, like his will to paint, had vanished that rainy day in the streets of Paris.

* * *

Samantha stared daggers at Maggie. "No way will I give into Jenice Anderson having anything to do with my brother," she stated flatly. "In the first place, she's Rebecca Morgan's sister. And in the second place, you saw the way she treated Bruce. I don't want her anywhere near Michael."

"I'm not sure who Rebecca Morgan is," Maggie admitted. "But I am aware of Jenice's connection with Bruce. Probably even more aware than you are, Sam."

Jason rolled his eyes. "Rebecca is the wife of Phillip Morgan," he explained to Maggie. "Phillip is a longtime friend of Bruce Vincent. Back when I was still playing Casper, I invited myself along on a date when Bruce took Sam to dinner at the Morgans'. Not only did Rebecca burn the duck she was roasting for dinner, she was the most obnoxious woman I've ever seen. She's a lawyer, and darned if she doesn't think that makes her a cut above the rest of us. After dinner she came up with a trivia game to show off her intelligence over a mere schoolteacher like Sam. But she underestimated Sam, who was doing just fine until Rebecca cheated. She started picking and choosing questions to fit her own skills and make the game harder for Sam. What she didn't reckon on was me. With my help, Sam tucked her in bed and turned out the lights."

Maggie listened carefully then turned to Samantha. "You're judging Jenice by her sister? That's hardly fair, is it?"

Samantha folded her arms tightly. "Blood is thicker than water," she huffed.

Maggie wasn't buying it. "You probably never heard of the man," she responded. "He didn't make the history books like his more famous brother, Christopher. But Alexander Columbus was so afraid of water he never even learned to swim. Get my point?"

"I get your point, Maggie. But I still don't like the woman, and there's nothing you can say to change my mind. And what do you mean, you're probably more aware of Jenice's connection to Bruce than I am?"

Maggie smiled, then went on to explain. "Do you remember the first time you were ever in this office?"

Samantha shrugged. "Sure I remember. I was on my way to marry Bruce when Gus caught me in the elevator. He handed me a contract, and explained it was to replace the one he had messed up with his typo. I read it and told him I wanted a few things changed.

When Gus saw that he couldn't talk me out of the changes, he put time on hold and brought me here. That's when we first met. And, I might add, the one and only time I can remember your computer making a mistake."

Maggie lifted her eyebrows. "You think my computer made a mistake, Sam?"

"I *know* your computer made a mistake, Maggie. I convinced Gus to find someone to take my place with Bruce, and Gus had one year to get Bruce a wife. We checked your computer, and it came up with the name of Jenice Anderson. It seemed okay to me at the time, but that was before I got to know the woman. She was rotten to Bruce and you know it, Maggie. You even helped me straighten out the mistake by bringing Arline into the picture. How can you think your computer didn't make a mistake?"

Maggie shook her head and smiled. "My computer didn't make a mistake, Sam. Jenice's name was given to us for reasons we didn't understand back then. She actually played a necessary role in getting Bruce and Arline together. Did you know that Bruce and Arline were contracted for each other the same as you and Jason?"

"They were?" Samantha asked with excitement. "That's great. But why did your computer put Bruce and Jenice together if Bruce had a contract with Arline?"

Maggie shook her finger at Samantha. "Let me finish, Sam. Arline and Bruce were contracted for each other, but unfortunately, neither had ever shown the slightest interest in the other. They knew each other through you, but Cupid's arrow had missed the mark with both of them. So, the higher authorities came up with Jenice Anderson. When Arline worked with Bruce to get Jenice back, she fell in love with him herself. Now Bruce and Arline are on their honeymoon, as you know."

Samantha was stunned. "You mean to tell me the higher authorities knew all along that I'd get involved when I saw Jenice mistreating Bruce? The higher authorities actually planned for me to bring Arline into the picture, knowing I'd do my best to shove Jenice out the door?"

Maggie looked at Samantha sharply. "For one thing, Sam, I don't think Jenice mistreated Bruce. I think she realized the two of them were wrong for each other, and gave Bruce the easiest way out possible. But as for the higher authorities knowing what you'd do, you bet they did. Right down to knowing who you'd pick for Jenice's replacement. You and Arline were best friends, remember?"

"All right, Maggie," Samantha conceded. "Your computer may not have made a mistake, but that doesn't raise Jenice one inch in my eyes. I don't like her, and I don't want her around my brother."

"Not even if it means saving your brother's life?" Maggie asked pointedly. "Do you have a better idea for someone Jason can prove himself to in a hurry?"

"No," Samantha admitted, her bottom lip protruding. "I don't."

"All right then," Maggie responded. "I'd suggest the two of you be on your way. You have an appointment with destiny on the decks of the cruise liner *The Wandering Star.*"

CHAPTER 4

Moving to the vanity mirror in her cabin, Jenice applied a fresh coat of lipstick. From the decks above, she could hear the band already in swing for tonight's open air dining and dance festivities. *What's the matter with you?* she thought, staring at her own reflection. *Why can't you relax and enjoy yourself? You turned down two invitations to the dance tonight, and both those guys were pretty cute. How long would it take you to get out of these jeans and into a dress? Get with it, woman. In less than twenty minutes you could be up there where the fun is.*

Saying these things to herself was easy; doing anything was something else. Sure, this cruise was an unexpected gift, but it wasn't something she'd asked for. Not that it wasn't a nice escape from the hubbub of the noisy newsroom. But something was definitely missing. Just like something was missing in everything she did for fun lately. The best she could expect out of this trip would be a boat ride, not a pleasure cruise.

Then again, it wasn't supposed to be a pleasure cruise. According to George Glaser, she was here to cover a story. What story? Good old George had been a little vague on that point. She still had no idea what the man was up to, but he definitely had something in mind. He always had something in mind when he put on his generous act.

"What sort of story am I looking for?" Jenice had asked when George sent her on this cruise. His answer still rang in her mind: "Hey, my tipster didn't say. Just keep your eyes open, Anderson. You're a reporter. You'll know a story when it pops up."

"Yeah, right," she said aloud. "Let's see, there was the woman who lost a pearl earring overboard while walking her dog on the upper deck this morning. Or maybe I could report on the ship's missing mascot. Believe it or not, readers, this seven-year-old parrot just came up missing right in the middle of a cruise. The parrot's name is *Gabby*, which doesn't make much sense when you realize the parrot has never said two words in its entire life. Several people were questioned by the ship's authorities concerning the matter, all of whom pleaded fowl play. The whole dreadful incident came to a close early this morning when Gabby was found hiding in a kitchen supply cabinet, munching down on what was left of a case of soda crackers."

Jenice flopped down crossways on the only chair in her cabin, and stared at the mini-chandelier hanging from the ceiling. "Now there is a press stopper if ever there was one. It should rate a two-inch headline, at least."

Something in the vanity mirror caught her eye. A quick look revealed the reflection of a man standing just inside her cabin door. Instantly, she spun to face the intruder. It occurred to her that his broad smile was very much out of place. Her first thought was that he was some sort of ship attendant, but she quickly dismissed this idea due to his casual dress. Ship personnel all wore uniforms. But if he was here to rob her, he certainly didn't look the part.

Maybe he was just a guy looking for a date, she thought. If so, he had picked the wrong way to introduce himself to this lady. Jenice was not one to put up with men who tried to push themselves on her–unless . . . ? Could it possibly be that this fellow represented the story that George said she would recognize when the time came?

"Who are you?" she asked guardedly. "What are you doing in my cabin?"

The fellow's smile grew even larger as he raised his shoulders in an exaggerated shrug. "Name's Jason," he said simply. "Jason Hackett."

Jenice stared hard at him. Reaching for a lamp off the vanity, she raised it up in a threatening position. "Well, Mr. Jason Hackett," she responded slowly, the words rolling out with deliberate sharpness. "You better have a good explanation for being in my cabin, and you had better give it to me fast if you don't want to find this lamp right in the middle of that smile you're wearing."

Jason shook his head and released a loud sigh. "You can't believe how I hate first introductions. I know you're going to find this hard to understand, Jenice, but I'm an angel."

"Yeah, right, and I'm an astronaut on my way to Jupiter. You've got just five seconds to turn yourself around and get out of my cabin before I get mad. And I warn you, you won't like me when I'm mad."

Jason knew he'd have to act fast. "I know my showing up in your cabin like this looks bad, but for someone in my position, there aren't too many alternatives. I am an angel though and I have proof."

Astonished beyond words, Jenice could only watch as the cabin was doused in brilliant light just as if an Independence Day rocket had exploded in the center of it. Gradually the light transformed into the shape of a luminous doorway in the corner of the room. It was then that she noticed the lamp was no longer in her hand, but was back on the vanity as it had been before she had grabbed it. While she was doing her best to assimilate this phenomena, an unseen force began pulling her toward the luminous doorway. Powerless to stop herself, Jenice could only close her eyes and hope for the best.

Within seconds, it was over. She opened her eyes and looked around her. She was standing on a sandy beach a few hundred feet from the breaking surf. She instantly recognized the place as Howard Placard's private beach. The same beach where six months before she had watched Bruce Vincent parachute from the sky. The same beach where she had met Arline Wilson for the first time and Arline had confessed that she was in love with Jenice's fiancé, Bruce. What a strange day that had been. Jenice caught her breath, remembering.

Jenice looked around her slowly. The intruder who had been in her cabin stood beside her on the beach. "What have you—how did you . . . ?"

"I told you," Jason said. "I'm an angel. I promised you proof. Well, how am I doing so far?"

"I must be—"

"No, Jenice," Jason responded patiently. "You're not dreaming. That's what you were about to say, isn't it? That's always the first question out of someone's mouth when I do something to prove myself."

"If I'm not dreaming, then I must be—oh my gosh—am I dead?"

Jason slapped the palm of his hand against his forehead. "No, you're not dead. Just once I'd like to have this go easy. I'll try to explain, okay? It looks like we're standing on the beach, but we're not really. This is what we angels call a Selected Event Shown by Holographically Enhanced Regeneration."

"A what?"

Jason didn't bother to repeat himself. "Just think of this whole thing like a movie and you're in a movie theater," he said. "Just imagine that I'm about to show a film clip of an old home movie, only it will feel a lot more real than a home movie."

Jenice swallowed hard and did her best to make some sense of this strange experience. Had she fallen? Bumped her head? Not that she could recall. Had she eaten something that might have upset her? Again, she could think of nothing. There had to be some logical explanation, and it probably boiled down to a trick of her mind.

That's what this had to be. A trick of her mind. It seemed real enough. It even felt real. Maybe if she just ignored this person he'd go away and she'd be back in her cabin where she belonged. On the other hand, maybe she should play along with the illusion. What could it hurt? If nothing else, she'd have a good laugh when she awoke. She decided to play out the hand and see what came of it.

"So . . . you really are an angel then?" she asked conversationally.

"Yeah," Jason responded. "I am. Jason Hackett's my name. I'm pretty sure you've heard of me. We know some of the same people."

She thought she had heard the name Jason Hackett, but where? As she forced herself to think, she suddenly remembered. "Arline Wilson," she gasped. "Jason Hackett is the same name Arline gave her imaginary angel."

Jason smiled with relief. "You got it, Jenice. Except for the imaginary part. And don't think Arline accepted me without a fight. She even called me a holograph. But in the end, look what I did for her image. Thanks to me, her ratings shot through the roof."

Jenice stared at Jason, wondering what was going on. *I'm really dreaming up a good one this time*, she thought. *Here I am on Howard Placard's beach, where I met Arline Wilson for the first and last time, and now I think I'm carrying on a conversation with her imaginary angel.*

Even though she'd already decided that this was just a dream, Jenice struggled to make sense of what she was hearing. "You have to understand, Jason Hackett, I'm still not a hundred percent sure you're real. But I'm going to go along with you for just a few minutes. First, let me ask you exactly what it is you want from me. And you need to know up front, I don't interview angels. Arline is a television talk show hostess, and talking with an angel did wonders for her. I, on the other hand, am a newspaper reporter. If I told anyone I talked to an angel, I'd end up on the cover of a tabloid faster than Monday morning's first rumor hits the streets."

"Slow down, Jenice," Jason cautioned her. "You're getting ahead of me here. I couldn't care less about an interview. What I have in mind is a lot more important. But first things first. I have a little show prepared that should prove once and for all that I'm telling the truth. What do you say we dive right in? Take a good look around, Jenice, and tell me if you recognize this place."

Jenice stared. "This appears to be Howard Placard's private stretch of beach. So tell me, what am I doing here?"

"How many times have you been here before?" Jason asked.

"I was here a couple of times. Once on a date with Bruce Vincent, and later on the day he parachuted from the sky. In fact, as I recall, Arline said that you were there, too."

Jason nodded. "So far, so good. Now, take a look at that brown Jeep over there in the parking lot. Look familiar?"

Jenice eyed the Jeep with astonishment. "That's my Jeep, and I believe that's just about where I parked it that day."

"Right on," Jason grinned. "Now take a look at who's sitting on that rock down near the water."

Jenice was almost afraid to look for fear she would see herself on the rock. Drawing a breath for courage, she turned to look. "It is me," she choked. "This is getting weirder by the second. What happens next? Does Arline show up like she did that day?"

Jason pointed back toward the parking lot. Jenice looked and spotted a green Toyota entering the lot. "It is Arline's car," she said. "So what's happening?"

"Everything you saw happen that day, and a bit more," Jason replied. "This playback was put together especially for you, Jenice. You're about to be shown something you couldn't see the day this actually happened. For example, look at the passenger side of Arline's car. Notice anything unusual?"

"Yes, I do. There's someone with Arline, another woman. But Arline was alone that day—although she did say something about having an angel around."

"Do you want to make a guess who the second woman is?" Jason asked.

Jenice raised her eyebrows. "I haven't a clue."

"All right, I'll give you a hint. She was engaged to Bruce before you were."

Jenice did a double take. "That's Samantha Allen?" she gasped. "I don't believe it. But wait—yes, I see it now. Bruce showed me a picture of her. She's even more beautiful than in her pictures. No wonder Bruce asked her to marry him."

Unseen to Jenice, the real Samantha stood next to Jason where she had been this whole time. "Humph!" she said in disgust. "All the flattering words in the world won't buy you one inch in my mind, Jenice Anderson. And besides, what you say is nothing but the truth."

Jason shook off Samantha's remark, but took this opportunity to make Jenice aware of her presence. "Just to bring you up to date, she later married yours truly. In fact, Jenice, she's standing right here next to me now."

"You're married to Samantha Allen? But how? Samantha is . . . But she's here, you say?"

Jason beamed. "Samantha is an angel, just like I am."

Jenice's face became very pale. "And you say she's here with you now? Why can't I see her? I can see you and you say you're an angel."

"Those are the rules, Jenice. You see me, and except in rare cases with special approval, one angel is all you're allowed."

Jenice looked back at the green Toyota. "But I can see her sitting in the car."

"That's because this playback was prepared especially for you since we needed a way of proving I'm really an angel in a hurry."

"Why?" Jenice looked at Jason curiously.

"Because Sam and I are faced with a small problem, and we need your help, Jenice."

Jenice looked disbelieving. "You need my help? You're supposed to be angels, and you need the help of a mere newspaper reporter?

Something doesn't add up here. I thought angels could do anything they liked without anyone's help."

Jason shook his head. "Wrong conception of angels, Jenice," he said briskly. "We have our limitations. Lots of them. Take my word for it—we do need your help, and that's why you're being shown this playback. By the time it's over, you should be a believer. If not, we could be facing a major problem."

Jenice was more confused than ever. More and more this whole crazy thing took on the look of being real. She glanced back to the parking lot where the green Toyota was just pulling to a stop next to her Jeep. The driver's door opened and Arline stepped out. Then Samantha—if that was who she really was—simply slid through the car door without bothering to open it.

"Did I see what I think I saw, Jason?" Jenice gasped. "I swear she slid through that door without bothering to open it."

Samantha rolled her eyes. "Brilliant deduction. We have ourselves a female Einstein here."

Forgetting for the moment that Jenice couldn't hear Samantha, Jason responded to his wife's remark. "Take it easy, Sam. I remember a few times when it used to bother you watching me walk through doors."

Suddenly realizing his mistake, Jason turned back to Jenice. "Oh, sorry about that. I was talking to Sam, here. But to address your concern, angels never bother opening doors. Not so long as we're visitors here in mortality, at least."

Jenice brushed a hand through her hair. "Never open doors, huh? Is that how you got in my cabin back on the ship?"

"You got it," Jason grinned. "Now what do you say we get a little closer to the women in the playback. It's important you hear their conversation."

Jason started off in the direction of the two women, and Jenice followed.

By this time, Jenice's curiosity had been teased enough to make her want to hear every word. As she and Jason followed the two women, Jenice grew quiet. It felt very strange, seeing a slightly younger version of herself, sitting on a rock not far away. As Arline pointed to the other Jenice and began speaking to Samantha, Jenice listened carefully.

* * *

"That's Jenice," Arline said, pointing. "I've never met her, but I recognize her from a picture Bruce carries in his wallet. I don't know which would be better—introducing myself, or waiting here until Bruce drops in."

"Let's go meet the woman," Samantha insisted. "It's always better to know everything you can about your competition."

"I suppose you're right," Arline agreed. "You will stay close to me though, won't you? Come to think of it, why isn't Jason here? Where is he, anyway?"

* * *

Jenice turned to Jason. "It seems so strange to see it from this perspective. I had no idea that Arline wasn't alone.

"Shh . . ." Jason said. "Listen." They watched as Arline and Samantha approached the rock where Jenice was seated.

* * *

"Hi," Arline said. "You must be Jenice Anderson."

"Yes, I'm Jenice," came the cautious reply. "But I'm afraid you have me at a disadvantage. Should I know you?"

"No, we've never met. My name's Arline Wilson. I'm a good friend of Bruce."

"Arline Wilson? From the radio show?

"One and the same. Have you heard my show?"

"Not for the last few weeks. But I used to listen to you regularly. You're a very talented woman, Arline, and I enjoy the variety of music your station plays. How do you know Bruce?"

"Bruce and I have been good friends for a very long time. He came to me for help when you gave him the challenge of jumping from the plane."

"Why would Bruce ask your help to learn skydiving?" Jenice asked. "Is it a hobby of yours, or something?"

"Actually, Jenice," Arline said matter-of-factly, "it wasn't Bruce's idea to come to me for help. It was my angel's idea. I only agreed to help out as a favor to the angel."

Jenice lifted her eyebrows. "Your angel asked you to help Bruce learn to skydive? I think there's more here than you're letting on, Ms. Wilson. Is your interest in Bruce somehow connected with your radio talk show?"

Arline shook her head. "No. My career has nothing to do with my interest in Bruce."

"If that's true, then why tie the angel to your association with him? Wait—" Jenice narrowed her eyes speculatively. "I think I can answer my own question. You have eyes for Bruce yourself, don't you?"

"I'd be lying if I said I didn't care for Bruce," Arline said. "But believe what you may, I only want what's best for Bruce. If that means stepping aside and letting him be part of your life, then so be it. But one thing I have to know before I can do that: are you really in love with him?"

"Am I in love with Bruce?" Jenice cocked her head to the side. "That's a little bit personal, wouldn't you say?"

"Yes, it is personal. But I don't want to see him hurt. I find it hard to believe you could give him an ultimatum like this skydiving thing if you really love him."

Jenice smiled ruefully. "I give you my word, Ms. Wilson, the last thing I want to do is hurt Bruce. To the contrary, I'm trying my best to spare his feelings."

"Trying to spare his feelings?" Arline asked sharply. "Why did you ever accept his ring in the first place if you didn't love him enough to be his wife? I'm sorry, but it doesn't sound like you're trying to spare his feelings at all."

Jenice rose from the rock where she had been sitting and walked over next to Arline. "You are in love with Bruce, aren't you?" she asked bluntly. "That's why you're so protective of him, isn't it?"

"Yes!" Arline snapped. "I admit it. I am in love with Bruce. But I do want what's best for him even if that means giving him up to you."

Jenice reached down and picked up a sea shell from the sand near her feet. For several seconds she studied the shell. Looking up from the shell, Jenice let her eyes meet Arline's. "Let me explain some things to you," she began. "I first met Bruce at the funeral of a previous fiancee. Her name was Samantha Allen. I'm sure you must have known Samantha, if you're a longtime friend of Bruce."

"I knew Sam," Arline quickly came back.

"My sister Rebecca pushed Bruce and me together from the first.

Bruce was heartsick at the time, and needed a friend. I decided that perhaps I could help him. After all, Bruce is an attractive man. But it took only a few dates to realize Bruce was not my type. Still, he was pleasant to be with.

"In the beginning it was my sister Rebecca who insisted I keep seeing him, but I have to admit that after a while I actually came to like Bruce. The major problem proved to be the difference in our lifestyles. Bruce is an easygoing, stay-at-home sort of man. I'm an adventuress. In time it became evident I would have to choose between Bruce, and my lifetime dream to go exploring. The choice wasn't an easy one, Arline.

"In the end I decided to hold onto my dream. I manufactured this skydiving scheme because I know Bruce well enough to know he could never go through with it. Instead of breaking off cold with him, I gave him a month to get used to the idea. At the same time I gave him the chance to see how impossible our relationship would be. Surely it's obvious to him by this time that the two of us are not compatible. If he can't parachute out of an airplane, how could he do the things I want from a husband? You ask me if I love him. Yes, I do. But like you, I want the best for him. And I'm sure that isn't me."

Reaching for Arline's hand, Jenice slid the sea shell she had been holding into it. "This shell," she said, "is very beautiful. I'm sure you're the sort of woman to enjoy its beauty. Unfortunately, I'm not one to enjoy it unless the creature is still alive to offer me the adventure of capturing it. The way it is now, I only had to reach to my feet and pick it up. I give you the shell, Arline. And I give you Bruce, as well. Both are very wonderful in their own way. Hold them close to your heart, and be happy."

* * *

By this time the holographic replay had Jenice's whole-hearted attention. She couldn't believe her eyes when the characters suddenly froze in place like statues in a wax museum.

"What are you doing, Jason?" she protested. "You can't stop now. I want to see the rest of this."

"Sorry, Jenice," Jason grinned. "That's all we had time to prepare."

"So that's it? You build my interest to the boiling point, then tell me that's all you prepared?"

"Hey, we were working under time constraints here," Jason defended himself. "The way we figured it, if this much didn't prove to you that I'm really an angel, nothing would. And since time is of the essence, we let it go at that. If you're dead set on seeing the rest of the scene, I'll work it up for you later on when we have more time. I'll even set you up with a special showing in a celestial theater–popcorn and all, okay? Right now we have other pressing problems to worry about. So are you convinced I'm real, or not?"

"All right, so I'm convinced," Jenice said. "But I'm not letting you off the hook on seeing the rest of the beach scene later on. Now what's this pressing problem you're so hot about?"

"Like I said, Jenice, we need your help—big time. A man's life is hanging in the balance."

Jenice's eyes widened. "A man's life is . . . ? And you need my help to . . . ?"

"We need your help to save his life, Jenice. And the worst of the problem is–we don't know when or where his life will be threatened. We only know the threat is real, and that it's destined to happen in the very near future."

Jenice threw up both hands. "You want me to save some guy's life, but you don't know from what? Or even when this—whatever—might happen? You're crazy, you know that?"

"I know what this sounds like, Jenice, but I'm telling you—the man is in real danger. I'm the only one approved to save him, and I can't do it without the help of a mortal assistant. We got all this information from a very sophisticated computer. And I know what you're thinking. But the computer files were partially locked, and we couldn't get any more details."

Jenice was quiet as she absorbed everything Jason had told her, then she said, "I have just this much to say, Jason Hackett. I don't know much about angels, but I would certainly have expected them to be a tad more organized than you seem to be. Do you even have any idea who this fellow is we're talking about, or where to find him?"

"Yes, we do know who he is," Jason asserted. "He's Sam's brother. And he's signed on as a passenger on *The Wandering Star*, same as you."

CHAPTER 5

The trip back to Jenice's cabin was much less spectacular than the one taking her to Howard Placard's beach. No bright lights, no sensation of being pulled through the door, none of these things. Just a simple here one second, there the next. One second the beach, the next her cabin.

Everything was just as she left it, including the lamp on the vanity that was burning brightly. "Okay," she said to Jason. "If you're limited to the things you said, how did you get the lamp back in its place?"

"I didn't," Jason admitted. "Gus' secretary, Maggie, took care of that part for me. She's also the one who put together the replay you just watched."

"She can do all that, but she can't save Sam's brother? Excuse my lack of understanding, but why?"

"The higher authorities," Jason responded. "Like I said, they decreed me as the only one approved for the job. And I need the help of—"

"A mortal," Jenice broke in. "And my name was picked out of the hat. By the way, why all the theatrics when we left here, and this simple zip-zap on the return? Are angels always this diverse in the way they do things?"

Jason's explanation was about what she expected. "The theatrics on the way to the beach were to get your attention, Jenice. You have to admit, it worked."

"Makes sense, I guess. By the way, is Sam still with us?"

"Not at the moment," Jason replied. "She's out scouring the ship for her brother so we can plan a strategy for getting the two of you introduced."

Something in the way Jason used the word "introduced" made Jenice start to wonder. Was there really a threat to Samantha's brother, or could this be an elaborate scheme to set her up with the guy? If there was one thing Jenice was not interested in at this time, it was becoming involved with a man. Cautiously, she pursued the thought with a simple question. "Sam's brother?" she asked. "Does he have a name? I can't remember you mentioning one." Whatever Jenice might have been thinking, she certainly wasn't ready for Jason's reply. It came like a shot of ice water right in her face.

"Sure he has a name, Jenice. It's Michael."

Jenice felt her knees go suddenly weak. "Michael?" she repeated feebly. "Michael Allen?" His last name was not difficult to figure since it had to be the same as Samantha's maiden name, which Jenice knew was Allen. She fell limp to the chair.

Jason stared at her, obviously caught off guard by the sudden change in her demeanor. "Yeah," he said. "That's his name. Michael Allen. Is something wrong, Jenice? All at once you don't look so good."

"All at once I don't feel so good, Jason." Reaching for her purse next to the chair, Jenice removed a wallet. Taking out a picture from the wallet she held it up for Jason to see. "Is this Sam's brother?" she asked, hoping against hope his answer would be no.

"That's Michael all right" came the words she didn't want to hear. "You know him, Jenice?"

All the color drained from Jenice's face as she returned the picture to her wallet and dropped the wallet back into her purse. "I know him," came her solemn response. "All too well, I'm afraid. This puts a whole new light on things, Jason. I'm not sure I can go through with our agreement. I'm not even sure I can finish this cruise knowing Michael is on board."

Jason rubbed a hand across his chin. "This doesn't sound good," he observed. "If it's any of my business, how do you know Michael?"

"It was two summers ago," Jenice explained. "I was vacationing in Paris with a couple of girlfriends. Michael and I met the first week I was there. Michael's father is in the Air Force." She glanced sheepishly up at Jason. "I guess you know that, don't you. I mean the man is your father-in-law."

Jason acknowledged with a nod and listened intently as Jenice continued. "Michael's father was on temporary duty in Paris at the time. Michael went there for a visit, and to do some painting. He's a great artist, you know. He sold four or five of his paintings in the short time I knew him."

Jenice swallowed hard, as the memories flowed clearly and painfully. "Michael and I spent the entire summer getting to know each other."

Jason was dumbfounded. "You and Michael spent a summer together? Oh boy, wait 'til Sam gets a load of this. But if the two of you are already friends, why all the doubts about helping him out now? That's even better, the way I see it."

"It goes a little deeper than our just being friends," Jenice went on. "Michael asked me to marry him."

"Asked you to—uh, oh. Sam's going to flip when she hears this. She's pretty protective of her brother, and . . ."

"Say no more, Jason. I understand. Believe me, I understand. Michael's a great guy, and if Sam thinks I mistreated Bruce when I turned him down . . ."

"Are you saying you turned Michael down too?"

"Yes, I did. Just like I did Bruce. I guess this makes me look pretty coldhearted, doesn't it?"

"Well, I think I can understand, but Sam . . ."

"I get the picture. I doubt it will help much, but I'll try to explain. I wasn't really in love with Bruce. I was on the rebound from Michael when I met him, and after giving my head time to clear I realized the two of us could never be compatible. With Michael, it was different. We had a great summer together, but his proposal caught me off guard. Marriage is something I'd never given much thought to. I have to admit, his offer was tempting. Oh, how it was tempting. I told him I needed some time to think it over. We agreed to meet in one week at the Eiffel Tower. I promised to have an answer for him by then.

"It was one of the hardest weeks of my life, Jason. Sort of like I was stuck in an elevator bouncing up and down between floors as people pushed buttons. One minute I was elated, and ready to take the plunge. The next, I wasn't so sure what I wanted. As the day drew near, I had practically decided to tell him yes. Then on the morning of the day I was to meet Michael, I received a call from George Glaser."

"George Glaser?" Jason asked. "An old boy friend?"

"George is my boss. Like I told you, I'm a newspaper reporter. George had a major story he wanted covered on the spot. It involved an interview with a Russian Air Force pilot, and it meant having the opportunity to ride in a Russian jet. George already had my flight plans arranged. I had barely an hour from the time he called to be on a plane bound for East Germany. You have to understand, Jason, giving up the chance to fly in a Russian jet was a pretty tough call for an adventure-loving lady like me. I tried phoning Michael, but I couldn't get through."

Jenice stood up and walked over to the mirror where she stood looking at herself a long time before continuing her story. "You'll never know how my heart ached when that plane lifted off the Paris runway," she said at last. "It was raining very hard that day. I could see the Eiffel Tower in the distance until we entered the clouds. I'm not sure what blurred it the worst, the rainsoaked window or my tears.

"I got my jet ride, Jason. Three of them, in fact. That Russian pilot even let me take over the controls a couple of times. It was one of the greatest thrills of my life. But it cost me. Believe me, it cost me. I've had a hard time looking myself in the eye ever since. And as for facing Michael again . . . I'm not sure I can go through with it."

"You have to go through with it," Jason insisted. "There's no telling what might happen to Michael if you refuse. Like I said before, someone a lot bigger than either of us has decreed we team up on this one."

Jenice stared at her image in the mirror. How could she ever face Michael again, after what she had done to him? But if she didn't face him, what then? What if he died and she could have saved him? Jason was right. She really had no choice.

* * *

The last rays of daylight were gone now, as Michael's attention remained glued to the Caribbean sky. A sky dotted with numberless glittering stars. Music from the far end of the ship reminded him that the evening's gala was in full swing. There was a time when he would have been happy to join the fun and laughter, but not now. It would only stir the embers of the flame, still burning from all the old memories. Instead he remained alone, drinking in the beauty of the evening sky.

At least he thought he was alone. How was he to know his blue-eyed, fair-haired sister was ever so near? Even beautiful angels are invisible most of the time.

"Hi, Michael," Samantha said cheerily, as though he could hear. "Why so sad, little brother? There's music and dancing at the other end of the ship, why not join them?"

"Oh, Sam," Michael whispered. "Why do I feel like you're here with me? You are here, aren't you? I just know it."

"Yes!" Samantha shouted excitedly. "I am here, Michael!"

Samantha knew that Michael could neither see nor hear her. But she also knew there was a chance he could feel her nearness. The same thing had happened with her cousins Julie and Lisa. They had both felt her presence, and even understood some things she said to them.

A shiver ran up Michael's spine as the feel of his sister's nearness grew even stronger. "If you are here, Sam, I want you to know how much I miss you. I spoke with Arline, you know. She told me she actually saw and talked with you. She even told me I have an angelic brother-in-law. What was his name—oh yeah—Jason. Jason Hackett."

"Yes, Michael, you do have a brother-in-law. You'd love him. He's a peach of a guy."

Michael laughed, and it felt good. Laughing was something he seldom did anymore. In life, his sister was always the one to cheer him up, and even if it was only in his heart she was doing it again.

"Arline told me how Jason courted you as an angel, and about how you made the choice to be with him. It helps, knowing all this, and that you're happy. Believe me, it helps. Just knowing you're out there somewhere makes missing you so much more bearable."

"You talked with Arline about me?" Samantha was surprised. She hadn't realized that her brother had ever talked to Arline. "Wow, that's neat. I want you to know I miss you, too. I sure wish I could have one of your hugs right about now."

Suddenly, Michael's attention was shifted from thoughts of his sister to a sinister figure near one of the lifeboats a hundred or so feet from where Michael stood. He strained for a better look. The man was mulling around nervously and holding what appeared to be a cloth bag so full that it was bulging at the seams. Strangest of all, the man was wearing a ski mask pulled down to cover his entire face. Michael moved quickly into the shadows and continued to watch.

The man moved to one of several lifeboats stationed there. Pulling back one edge of the canvas covering, he shoved the cloth bag inside the lifeboat. Michael looked on in astonishment as the man disengaged the safety mechanism that secured the lifeboat in place. The man didn't lower the boat to the water just yet, even though that had to be his intent for releasing the safety latch. Michael could only assume he was preparing the boat for a fast get-away later on.

No doubt about it—this fellow was up to no good, and Michael was probably the only one who knew about it. Reason told him he should mind his own business, but how could he do that in good conscience? For Michael Allen, there was only one answer to that question. Stepping out from the shadows, he approached the man. Gathering his courage, he spoke. "Excuse me, sir. Would you mind explaining why you're wearing the ski mask?"

The fellow spun to face Michael. "Wha— who are you?" he snapped, startled by Michael's unexpected intrusion. "Why are you wandering the decks when there's a party going on?"

"I felt like being alone. But you didn't answer my question. Why the mask?"

"The mask is none of your business, pal. Why don't you take a hike?"

Michael glanced at the bag in the lifeboat. It was lying on its side, and some of the contents had spilled out. A closer look revealed a watch and a few other items of jewelry. "This doesn't look good, fellow," he said. "Offhand I'd say you've been visiting some of the passengers' cabins while they're at the party. I think you and I had better have a little talk with the captain."

"Blast you, man!" the fellow cried out. "I'm part of the show, and you're spoiling my act. Why did you have to show up, anyway?"

"Part of the show?" Michael asked. "Maybe so, maybe not. We'll ask the captain when we see him." Michael reached out and took the man by the arm. "Come on, let's go for a little walk. What do you say?"

In a flash, the man reached inside his vest and came out with a light caliber revolver, which he pointed at Michael. "No!" he insisted. "I'm not letting you do this. You leave me no choice but to lock you in a cabin until the show's over."

Michael extended a hand. "You don't want to do this, mister," he stated calmly. "Stealing is one thing, but assault with a deadly weapon and kidnapping will get you in big trouble. Just put the gun down and let's talk this over, okay?"

"I can't do that!" the man shouted, more nervous than ever. "I have some rope in my cabin; I'll just have to tie the door shut. Oh my gosh, I can't do a thing like that. What am I going to do? I can't let you spoil my show."

* * *

Jenice was still staring at herself in the mirror. All the reasoning in the world couldn't lighten the dread of what she knew had to be done. If Michael's life was in danger, as Jason explained, she had no other course than to warn him. Warn him? But how? Neither she, nor Jason had any hint of where the danger would come from. Or when. Jason seemed willing to trust the higher authorities, as he called them, to work out the details. She would just have to take a lesson from him and do the same. She shifted her stare from her own image to Jason. Instantly, she knew something was wrong. The look on his face left little doubt.

"What is it, Jason?" she quickly asked.

"Sam's back," he responded. "She found Michael, and he's already in big trouble. Some man in a ski mask is holding him at gunpoint on the aft deck."

Suddenly, all dread of coming face to face with Michael vanished. In its place came a concern strong enough to send her mind spinning for answers. "Where on the aft deck?" she asked, already half way to the cabin door.

"Sam will lead the way," Jason shouted. "Follow us."

Jenice paused long enough to grab her purse, thinking it might be a good weapon, then shot out the door and up the stairs toward the top deck. Jason stayed just ahead of her.

Dashing out of the stairwell onto the deck, she turned aft and ran as fast as her legs would carry her. Then, she spotted them. She stopped for a moment to stare at the scene before her. Her heart leapt from within as reality revealed the truth: this really was Michael. The scene before her was even more frightening than she had supposed it would be. But neither Michael, nor his assailant had seen her yet, and that was good.

In an instant, she had moved up behind the assailant. Then, with one harsh swing of her purse, she sent him sprawling to the floor, where he lay moaning in pain. Without hesitation, she leaned down and picked up the pistol which had fallen from the man's hand.

All of this was the easy part. Now came the moment she dreaded most. Ever so slowly she turned to face Michael. Their eyes met, and her legs became like Silly Putty. "Hello, Michael," she said, her lip quivering noticeably. Then, trying to lighten things up a bit, she added, "You're looking good for a man who was about to be shot."

Michael's jaw lowered, and it was several seconds before he could respond. "Jenice," he asked in disbelief. "But how—that is—what are you doing on board this ship?"

Samantha gasped. "You two know each other? Wait just a minute here. No one bothered telling me this part."

Jason bit down on a finger while trying to decide whether or not to speak up. What the heck, the problem wasn't going to disappear anyway. "You don't know the half of it, Sam," he cringed. "Not yet, anyway."

"I don't what?" Samantha rumbled, staring at Jason through narrowed eyes. "What do you know that I don't, my cute little ghost?" Before he could answer, Jenice spoke.

"I'm sorry about Paris, Michael. It was cruel of me, I know. I tried to telephone you, but—"

"Paris?" Samantha grimaced. "They knew each other in Paris? Do something, Jason. She's saved Michael's life, so let's find a way to get rid of her—now!"

"I'd like to explain, if you'll let me," Jenice went on to say. "Not that it matters, I suppose, but I would like the chance to tell you what happened."

Michael was about to respond when he noticed the man in the mask struggling to get back on his feet. "Oh my head," the fellow groaned, with a hand to his crown. "What did you hit me with, anyway?"

Michael took the pistol from Jenice. "Don't try any more funny stuff," he warned. "Like it or not, you and I have an appointment with the captain. I think he'll be glad to learn what you've been up to."

"I've already met the captain," the man moaned. "He happens to be my older brother."

"The captain is your brother?" Michael asked in confusion. "And you're robbing the passengers on his ship?"

"I'm not robbing anybody. I tried to tell you before. I'm an actor."

The man reached up and removed the mask revealing a mild-looking individual in his mid-thirties with a rather large lump on his partially bald head. "My brother, the captain, hires me for all his cruises. I'm part of the entertainment for the evening's festivities. I play the part of a robber. The security patrol supposedly catches me in the act; I'm arrested and brought to light in front of the whole ship's audience. Then I pull my gun and make a fake getaway in this lifeboat. That's when the passengers are let in on the gag, and I'm brought back aboard to the sound of their wild applause. Now thanks to you and your girlfriend with the anvil in her purse, things are all fouled up. You've ruined everything. I hope you're happy."

"Yeah, right," Michael said suspiciously. "You're an actor. That's why you pulled this pistol on me. I'm sorry, pal. I'm not buying it. We're talking with the captain, who I doubt very much is your brother."

"That gun doesn't have real bullets in it. For crying out loud, what do you take me for? It's loaded with blanks. Let me have it, and I'll show you."

"Just hold it right there!" Michael warned. "I'll check the gun for myself."

The fellow took a step backward. "Go ahead. Snap open the cylinder. You'll see."

Michael released the catch with his thumb and flipped the gun to one side, causing the cylinder to pop open. Pulling out one cartridge, he examined it. "You're right," he conceded. "This is a blank. But what about these jewels?"

"All fakes. The whole sack is worth less than twenty bucks."

"Wait a minute," Samantha paused. "If that gun is loaded with blanks . . . ?"

Jason finished her sentence for her. "It means Jenice didn't really save Michael's life after all. And it means he's probably still in danger."

At that very moment something so unexplainable occurred, it caught everyone present by surprise. A sudden gust of powerful wind struck from out of nowhere, tearing loose the canvas tarp from the nearby lifeboat, sending it flying into the darkness of the night. Jenice fought to hold her footing, but soon lost the battle. Before she knew what hit her, she was hurled into the lifeboat along with Michael, who had been standing next to her when the turmoil began.

The force of two bodies falling against the lifeboat dislodged it from its mounting and sent it crashing into the cold Caribbean waters.

By the time Jenice was able to regain her senses, the lifeboat was adrift and had already moved several yards away from the mother ship. Her first thought was to cry out for help. But who would hear? Most of the passengers were at the far end of the ship, where the noise of the band would most certainly drown out a distress call.

She quickly looked for the would-be robber, only to discover he was in a bit of a predicament himself. While he had somehow managed to avoid falling into the lifeboat, he had nevertheless become tangled up in the rigging. He dangled a few scant feet from the surface of the water, clinging to the rigging for dear life.

With a sinking heart, Jenice watched the gap between the lifeboat and the cruise liner grow rapidly wider. As if all this wasn't bad enough, even Jason had seemed to have abandoned her in this moment of distress. He was nowhere to be seen. *Well,* she reasoned in her befuddled mind, *you wanted an adventure, lady. It looks like you got your wish, doesn't it?*

* * *

"What was that?" Samantha gasped, as she gathered her wits about her. "What pushed them into the lifeboat?"

"I don't know," Jason admitted. "I've never seen anything like it. It can't be natural. There's not even a trace of wind tonight."

"Something else is wrong, too," Samantha observed. "I can't make myself move to the lifeboat. Every time I try, I feel like my feet are glued to the deck. Do something, Jason. I don't want Jenice left alone in that boat with my brother."

"I'm trying to do something. I can't move that way, either. Something very strange is going on here, Sam. In my twenty-plus years as an angel, this has never happened to me. All I can figure is that whoever's playing games with Maggie's computer must be carrying things a step further."

All Samantha could do was watch as the little craft carrying her brother and Jenice drifted further and further out into the deep, black waters of the Caribbean. She had never felt so helpless in her life. Not as a woman, and certainly not as an angel.

CHAPTER 6

Not all that far away, a man was walking along the shore of his little island, something he loved to do every night at sunset. It was always a peaceful time . . . .

"Ye be a stubborn one, Brad Douglas, that's what ye be . . ."

Yes—and once in a while his thoughts were interrupted by a certain ghost who liked to show up unannounced every now and then.

"Are we back to this conversation again?" Brad asked, a little disappointed at the interruption of his leisurely walk. "You know my feelings on the matter. If either of us has cause to walk away from this island, it's you, old friend. Not me."

"Aye, ye be a stubborn one all right. Stubborn enough to drive a man to the rum barrel—a habit, by the way, that the likes of meself never saw fit to indulge in. But by the stars, ye not be stubborn enough to drive Captain Horatio Symington Blake off his own island."

"*Your* own island? It's back to that again now, is it? I've told you a thousand times, Blake, this island is not your personal haunting ground. It's as much mine as it is yours. Why can't you accept that?"

"Tummy rot! This here was my island before ye set one foot on its soil, and unless things change, it'll be mine long after yer last dyin' breath lies cold on these here salty airs. Those be me final words on the subject, matey."

Brad threw up his hands in disgust. "You have the gall to call me stubborn. I'll tell you what stubborn is. Stubborn is a hard-headed, belligerent, completely-devoid-of-common-sense ghost who's too blasted proud to set one foot through the wide open door waiting to take him home. Here you stay, haunting this desolate piece of volcanic rock when your friends and family alike are pleading with you to join them on the other side. And they're right, you know. The other side is where you belong. Staying here like this is pure nonsense. And that, my old friend, is a true definition of what stubborn is all about. If stubborn had a patent, you'd have the rights tied up solid."

"Blast ye, man!" the captain shot back. "Ye know why I stay on this here side of the line. Capt'n Blake is not one to go back on his word. I gave me word, and by thunder, I'll be keeping me word."

Brad stared at his old friend, wishing for a way to break through the wall of self-constructed pride that surrounded the old sea captain. But after three centuries of adding to the wall, it was a little difficult to penetrate by this time. The sad truth was that Blake had only to say the word, and one very anxious celestial greeter would escort him home in the batting of an eye. But would he say the word? Ha! No chance of that. Not with this ridiculous hang-up about getting a worthless map in the hands of a bloodline descendant of Oscar Welborn, he wouldn't.

Brad listened while the captain continued. "Ye call me stubborn for not castin' sail to a finer life? What about you, Brad Douglas? If either of us should be thinkin' of a world outside this cursed strip of rock, it be you. And don't be arguin' with me, matey. Ye know I speaks the truth on the matter."

The captain was right, Brad did know life could be more comfortable for him as well. There were times he longed to go back home. But—it just wasn't to be. Sometimes it didn't seem possible that ten years had passed since he first set foot on this island. Where had all the time gone? And the most intriguing question of all, what would things be like back at the old home front now? Would Lori still be there? Would she be happy with the man she had chosen over Brad? Were there any children? Lori would make a great mother, no question about that. If only . . .

Brad let out a lingering sigh. Lori was history now. And if she was married and had children, they would belong to another man. Thinking about Lori now was something better left alone. For that matter, all thoughts of home were futile at this point. And they would be as long as James Baxter was in the picture.

James Baxter. The sound of his name alone was enough to give Brad cold chills. If only his sister, Shannon, had listened to Brad all those years ago and had never married that evil man. Then none of this would have ever happened.

Poor Shannon. Even after she had married James Baxter, she couldn't get it through her head that his fits of rage weren't her fault. It was always the same. Once the rage had passed, Baxter would beg for her forgiveness, promising that it would never happen again.

"He needs me," Shannon used to tell Brad. "I know if I try hard enough, I can learn to please him. I'll just try a little harder next time. If I can just do that, everything will work out, you'll see."

The fact that Baxter was a moderately wealthy man, with suspected ties to the underworld didn't help matters, either. All the more reason why Shannon should fear him.

Shannon was sure that after Tanielle was born, Baxter would change. And change he did. The problem was, his change was not for the better. It took five more years of the worst abuse imaginable before Shannon found the courage to walk away from the man. And unfortunately, that courage had come only as a result of what had happened on Tanielle's fifth birthday. When Baxter walked in the house that night and saw that Shannon had spent money on a cake and a pretty doll for Tanielle, he had lost his temper completely. Shannon would probably have forgiven him for shoving cake in her face, if he had only stopped there. But in his rage, he backhanded Tanielle so hard it sent her crashing to the floor, chair and all. It was the first time he had ever struck his daughter. Shannon left him on the spot, or at least she tried. As usual, Baxter had other ideas.

To Baxter's way of thinking, Shannon had no rights of her own. She was his property, to do with as he pleased. When he refused to leave her alone, she took the matter before a judge who issued a restraining order, which Baxter ignored. Words—locks—law officers—nothing seemed capable of keeping him from hounding her. Nothing, that is, until Brad stepped in and took charge of things.

Brad planned everything out to the smallest detail, and he kept his plan under the tightest of wraps. No one, except Shannon and Tom Reddings knew what he was up to. An old friend of their father, Tom was an Air Force pilot.

Their escape took place in the dead of night. With Tom's help, Brad, Shannon, and Tanielle were loaded onto an Air Force cargo plane bound for the U.S. Virgin Islands. By the time the sun came up the next morning, they were on the island of Saint Thomas. Three short days later, they had taken up residence on this tiny island. An island felt by most to be uninhabitable. But with a motivation like theirs, proving everyone wrong was paramount. And—they succeeded.

It wasn't easy, at first. They had to live in tents until Brad was able to construct a house. It was while he was building the house that he first met Captain Blake. Now there was something that took a little getting used to. From the time they first arrived at Saint Thomas, Brad had heard the stories about a ghost haunting this small island, but he put little stock in the matter. That is, until he found himself the prime target of Captain Blake's haunting escapades.

At first, the old sea captain didn't like Brad, and he let him know it. Blake felt the island belonged to him and that Brad and the others were unnecessary intruders who should be frightened off like everyone else who had set foot on his island over the last three centuries. However, it didn't take long for Captain Blake to realize he had met his match in this newcomer, and that's when their friendship first took root. A friendship that had grown, over the years, into one of mutual respect and admiration.

Brad's brief moment of reminiscing was broken by the sound of the captain's voice. "With the sharks as me witness, it makes me no never-mind that Oscar Welborn be in the world of angels now. And it makes me no mind that Oscar, gentleman that he is, stands willin' to let me off of me promise. I gave me word, and when Cap'n Blake gives his word, his word be kept. I'll not be leavin' this island until a descendant of Oscar Welborn has in his hands the map that shows where the lady lies, on the bottom of the Atlantic. These be me words, and me words be the law."

Brad drew a breath of salty air and stared at his old friend. "You know," he said. "You never have told me anything about this lady you talk about all the time. What if you do ever run into one of Welborn's descendants? What's so all-fired important about this lady that would tempt them to dredge her off the bottom of the Atlantic Ocean?"

"Aye, ye said it yerself," Blake responded, with a squint in his left eye that was so much his manner. "I never told ye about the lady, and

I never will. That's a secret I be keeping til I come face to face with one proven to be blood kin to old Oscar."

Brad shook his head in disgust. "Well if you're so dead set on hanging around this old world until you find this person, why in reason's name don't you go looking for him—or her—as the case may be? Do you think this person will just suddenly show up here on this island? Use your head, Blake. It's not going to happen."

"That, me proud matey, is where ye be wrong. I've been talkin' with me friend, Gus. He says the time will come when the very person I be waitin' for will be brought right here to this very island."

Gus, Brad knew from his earlier conversations with the captain, was the fellow who kept in touch with Captain Blake from the other side. Although Brad had never seen Gus himself, he had no reason to doubt the captain's word about him.

The captain continued. "Aye, it seems Gus is treadin' deep waters over the likes of me stayin' here on this side these three centuries. It be not a natural act, and the rules have been somewhat bent in me case. Them he refers to as 'the higher authorities' have presented him an ultimatum to be solvin' me case and gettin' me home where they say I belong. Old Captain Blake has Gus over a barrel, matey, and Gus be promisin' to have the person I be waitin' for on me island in the very near future. So, ye see, ye may be gettin' yer wish about me crossin' over to the other side sooner than ye may think."

Brad wanted to believe his friend's prediction of a happy ending to his dilemma, but what were the chances of it ever happening? This Gus, whoever he was, would have to pull some pretty big strings to even find a descendant of Oscar Welborn, let alone get him here to this island. No, the chances of either Captain Blake or Brad leaving this island anytime soon were slim to none.

The cool water of an unexpected wave washed smoothly over Brad's bare feet, bringing a smile to his face. What was he complaining about, anyway? Here he was, living a life of leisure in a tropical paradise. He knew most people only dreamed of such things; instead they awoke every morning to the sound of an alarm clock beginning another nine-to-five day at the work place. *Get real, Brad Douglas,* he told himself. *You've never had it so good.*

CHAPTER 7

It took only minutes for *The Wandering Star* to vanish into the darkness of the night, leaving the tiny lifeboat adrift in the lonely waters of the Caribbean Sea. The last sounds of the ship's band faded into a chilling silence so thick it could almost be felt. For a long time, Jenice stared where she'd last seen the ship. How had all this happened, anyway? The unexpected cruise, the phenomenal appearance of Jason Hackett, the man in the ski mask, a totally unexplainable force throwing her into this lifeboat—there was no logical reason behind any of it.

But the thing that weighed heaviest on her mind was not that she was adrift in a lifeboat; it was that she was adrift in a lifeboat with Michael Allen as her sole companion. How could fate be so cruel? She glanced at Michael, only to see him looking back. As their eyes met, a cold chill shot through her.

It was Michael who spoke first. "I don't suppose you'd like to explain all of this, would you, Jenice?"

His question caught her totally unprepared. "I don't know what you mean, Michael. Explain what?"

"For one thing, I'd like to know why you pushed me into this lifeboat."

"I pushed you? Is that what you think? Why would I do a thing like that?"

Michael glared at her. "This whole thing was a setup, wasn't it, Jenice? The guy in the mask, the make-believe robbery, the gun—you planned it all, didn't you? Then you came along with your put-on rescue act, trying to make it look like you saved me from being kidnapped. Did you really think I'd fall for such a gimmick? But what I don't understand is why. What possible motive could you have for getting the two of us together in this lifeboat? If it's because you wanted to talk things out, why not just meet me somewhere for dinner? Not that it would matter, anyway. There's really nothing left for either of us to say. You made your intentions pretty clear back in Paris."

For once in her life, Jenice was at a loss for words. What could she possibly say to defend herself? *You see, Michael, this angel came to me with the story that you were in danger so I just naturally agreed to help with your rescue.* Sure, that's what she could tell him. She could even tell him it was the angel who undoubtedly pushed the two of them into this lifeboat. Sure, he'd believe her, Jenice snorted to herself. Why shouldn't he believe her? She'd only broken his heart and disappeared from his life without a word.

Futile as the effort seemed, she gave it her best shot. "Look, Michael. You can believe what you will, but the fact is I had nothing whatsoever to do with any of this. I'm just as confused as you are how we ended up in a lifeboat."

"You're right about one thing, Jenice. I can believe what I will. I believed you once, back in Paris. All I got for my trouble was soaking wet from standing in the rain."

Michael's words cut like a razor. "I admit, what I did was wrong, Michael," she said softly. "I hurt you and I'm sorry. But I am telling the truth now. I had nothing to do with any of this."

Michael paused to consider what Jenice was saying before issuing a challenge. "Look me straight in the eye and tell me this is none of your doing. Can you do that, Jenice?"

Jenice looked him in the eye. "I had nothing to do with this, Michael. I am telling the truth."

Michael paused again. Then, to Jenice's relief, said, "You really are telling the truth, aren't you? I can see it in your eyes."

Jenice had to blink and look away. Their eyes were joined only for a moment, but it was long enough for the old feelings to flourish, feelings best left safely tucked away in the folds of protected memories. "Yes, Michael. I am telling the truth. Your accusations are way out of line. How we got in this lifeboat is just as big a mystery to me as it is to you. But, since we're here, I suggest we take a close look at our situation. There's no telling how long we may be in this boat, and it would help to have a plan."

Michael nodded. "I agree. There are compartments on the sides of the boat. Why don't we find out what's in them?"

Jenice opened the compartment closest to her and did a quick inventory. "Let's see, we have a flashlight, some two-gallon containers of fresh water, several blankets and—hey, we won't go hungry. We have some cans of Spam, some dried fruit, and even some chocolate bars. Wow, are we uptown, or what?"

"I've got a dozen or so life jackets on this end," Michael said. "That should be enough, I would think. And here's something we can definitely use—a set of oars."

"Oars?" Jenice laughed. "Oh, wonderful. I have just one question—which way do we row? All I see is water in every direction."

"Don't look at the water," Michael directed. "Look at the sky."

Jenice glanced upward. The view was breathtaking. A full moon lay near the edge of the horizon while the rest of the sky was filled with more stars than she could ever remember seeing.

"Okay," she said. "I'm looking at the sky. I don't see any arrows pointing to the closest patch of dry land."

"Over there," Michael said, pointing just off the edge of the Big Dipper. "That's the North Star. All we have to do is put our right shoulder to it and head due east."

"You sound pretty sure of yourself," Jenice said.

"I have a good idea where we are," he defended himself. "Just before dark I noticed the island of Vieques off to the north. Vieques is situated just at the eastern tip of Puerto Rico. Since *The Wandering Star* was moving west, we can backtrack to the east. Even if we miss Vieques altogether, we're bound to run into the larger island of Puerto Rico."

Jenice thought a moment. "I don't know," she countered. "If you saw Vieques to the north, that must mean South America is to the south. Maybe we should head that way. It is a bigger target, you know."

Michael shook his head. "I admit the mainland's a bigger target, but we're a lot closer to Puerto Rico. I vote we go east."

Jenice nodded. "Okay, we'll do it your way. But if you foul up and get me stuck in the South Atlantic, you're going to hear about it."

Michael dropped the oars into the water with the intention of turning the boat due east. After struggling without success for several minutes, he rested on the oars and looked at Jenice. "I don't get it," he said. "I can't turn the boat around. It's like something has hold of us, pulling us toward the northwest. I wouldn't think the currents would be this strong in the Caribbean."

"But that will take us toward the Atlantic, won't it?" Jenice asked, frowning.

"It will if we miss the Virgin Islands. And if you thought Puerto Rico was a small target . . ."

"How about if we both get on the oars, Michael. Do you think we can turn the boat around then?"

"I really don't think so. Whatever has hold of us is doing a good job keeping our heading where it wants us to go." Michael shrugged his shoulders and laughed. "I know this sounds crazy, but it's almost like some unseen force is in play here."

"An unseen force?" Jenice asked in disbelief. "We're in the Caribbean, Michael, not the Bermuda Triangle."

"I said it sounded crazy, didn't I? But I'm telling the truth. I can't turn this boat around."

"That doesn't seem very fair," Jenice said. "It's okay for you to have an unseen force pulling the boat the wrong way, but when something just as strange tosses you into this boat—you suspect me of pushing you. I think you owe me an apology, Mr. Allen."

"I already said I believed you about not pushing me," Michael said. He frowned and scratched the back of his head. "But you do raise an interesting point. It is almost like some invisible force threw us in this boat, and now the same sort of thing is pulling us where we don't want to go. Maybe the Bermuda Triangle isn't the only place where weird things happen."

Taking a deep breath, Jenice made a decision. "At the risk of making you think I'm really somewhere in outer space, let me tell you the whole story about what happened back there on *The Wandering Star*. How do you think I showed up just when your buddy in the ski mask pulled a gun on you, Michael? Did you wonder about that at all?"

Michael looked surprised. "No, I guess I didn't. So lay it on me. How did you happen by at the precise moment?"

Jenice didn't answer immediately. Instead, she dipped the ends of her fingers in the water, then pulling her hand out, she watched as one by one the drops fell back into the sea. "This isn't easy for me, Michael," she began, never taking her eyes off her hand. "But let me ask you a question. Do you believe in angels?"

* * *

Samantha paced the floor of Maggie's office while Jason looked on sympathetically.

"What am I going to do, Maggie?" she asked nervously. "Michael needs my help. He's out there somewhere on that ocean, and I can't stand the thought of leaving him alone with that woman. How am I ever supposed to find him when all the information your computer will cough up is the name of some dead sea captain? This is crazy. I thought being an angel meant never having this sort of problem."

"I've explained about my computer," Maggie reminded Sam. "Your file is locked. I did my best to learn what's in store for Michael, and all it would produce is the name Captain Horatio Symington Blake. That, and a brief note saying the captain is part of Michael's immediate future. And as for angels never having problems, where did you ever get such a crazy idea, Sam? Problems are forever. Gus is not exempt from problems, I'm not exempt, and I suspect even the higher authorities have their fair share."

"I don't know, Maggie," Samantha sighed. "I just sort of supposed those things were behind me when I became an angel."

Maggie laughed. "Not hardly. Becoming an angel is only the beginning of a very long and very rewarding road on this side of forever. I'm looking forward to my next stop along the way. But each step comes only when we're prepared, and we prepare by having experiences. You know what they say about experience, don't you, Sam?"

Samantha shook her head.

"They say experience is what you get when you don't get what you wanted."

"Yeah, right," Samantha grumbled. "Like having your brother lost at sea with the last woman on earth you'd ever want him with."

Maggie smiled. "Everything will work out fine, Sam. You'll see. Just have a little patience."

"Patience?" Samantha groaned. "Maggie, you know I hate it when people tell me to have patience. When something needs doing, get it done—that's my motto."

"Sometimes the higher authorities require us to have patience, Sam," Maggie said consolingly. "Who knows, maybe that has something to do with the experience you're facing now."

Samantha's face went hot. "Are you suggesting that the higher authorities cooked up this little game to teach me patience?"

Maggie shrugged. "It's just a suggestion, Sam. After all, you're an accomplished schoolteacher. Haven't you ever set up a situation that would allow a student to have an experience that would teach him what he needed to learn?"

Samantha hated it when she found herself backed into a corner, like now. But Maggie was right. There were many times she had used experience as a teaching tool. Still, admitting she needed a lesson in patience was another thing. She changed the subject by asking a question, "Who is this Captain Horatio Symington Blake anyway?"

"Let me answer that," Jason interrupted. "I can tell you who Captain Blake is."

All eyes shifted to Jason. Samantha was ready to pounce in with her own question, but since Maggie beat her to the punch, she opted to listen and learn. "You know Captain Blake?" Maggie asked.

"Yeah, sorta," Jason said. "I met him once several years ago. It wasn't long after an experience of my own, the one with the chicken bone. I was a greenhorn angel and Gus was sticking pretty close to me. I even tagged along on a few of his assignments."

"Gus took you along on a visit with Captain Blake?" Maggie pressed further.

"Yes, and talk about a hardheaded character. Poor Gus has had his hands full with that guy."

"Let me guess," Maggie said. "Gus was trying to talk Captain Blake into coming over to our side of the line, right?"

"He was trying, but he wasn't having much luck. Blake kept going on about some map he had to get in the hands of the blood descendant of a guy he called . . . let me think . . ." Jason paused, trying to remember.

"Oscar Welborn?" Maggie volunteered.

"Yeah, that's the guy. The map supposedly showed the location of his sunken ship. And he kept mentioning something about a lady. I never did catch the point on that one."

Maggie looked strangely worried. "Gus never mentioned you meeting Captain Blake," she said. "It must have slipped his mind. Do you remember, by chance, where Gus took you to meet the captain?"

Jason thought a moment. "It was on a little island. But to tell the truth, Maggie, I paid so little attention at the time that I can't remember where it was exactly. I think it was part of the Virgin Islands, but . . ."

Samantha looked up suspiciously as Maggie's smile returned. Something in her demeanor seemed very strange.

"Good," Maggie said with a satisfied look on her face. "Uh . . . I mean, that's good you know Captain Blake, not that you can't remember where the island is, I mean. Captain Blake died a little over three hundred years ago. And just as you observed, he refuses to leave the island where he's been ever since. In his mind, he has some unfinished business that has to be taken care of before he'll consider giving up his self-declared vigil."

"One thing I don't understand," Jason said. "It didn't seem like Gus had been working with the captain all that long. The guy's been dead more than three centuries. What's the deal?"

Maggie appeared happy to explain. "Captain Blake's case was originally assigned to Walter Stone, the Special Problems Coordinator over the department that handles out-of-the-ordinary situations, like the captain's."

"So, how did Gus get involved if the guy wasn't his problem?"

Maggie rolled her eyes. "You know Gus. He's always working some angle. He offered to take the captain off Walter's hands in exchange for one of his own problem cases. You see, Jason, Gus' typo that sent your life out of kilter wasn't his only goof-up. He's managed a few more over the centuries. In this case it was a client destined to be born in Denver, Colorado, with the first name of John. Gus mistakenly sent him into the world—right in the middle of Hong Kong, China, where his name came out Wong."

"You mean 'wrong,' don't you?" Jason laughed.

Maggie joined in his laughter. "It was Wong, and you're right. It was wrong, too."

"It figures," Jason groaned. "Knowing Gus he probably reasoned that since Colorado and China both start with the letter 'C', one should be as good as the other."

"Don't ask me to explain his mistake," Maggie continued. "But so help me, that's what happened. And as you can probably guess, Beverly—the lady Wong was destined to meet—was still in Denver. Bottom line, Gus traded his Wong problem for the captain, thinking he was putting one over on Walter. But Walter managed to wrap things up very neatly. He simply arranged for Wong to go to Denver as an exchange student. There he met Beverly, and as you probably guessed, the two hit it off right away. Captain Blake's problem, on the other hand, is still on the burner."

None of this came as any surprise to Samantha, knowing Gus as she did. One thing still puzzled her, however. It was the way Maggie had acted when she thought Jason might know the whereabouts of Captain Blake's island. Samantha had had her suspicions from the time Maggie first complained about her computer files being locked up. Did Maggie know more than she was letting on? The way Samantha saw it, there was only one way to find out.

"Correct me if I'm wrong, Maggie," she said. "But are you saying that this Captain Blake is on an island somewhere in the Caribbean Sea?"

Maggie hesitated. "I didn't say *where* the island was, Sam. Jason was the one who mentioned the Caribbean."

"All right then, Maggie, let me ask you point blank. Is Captain Blake's island in the Caribbean Sea?"

Maggie looked reluctant to answer. "What are you getting at, Sam? What makes you think I even know where the island is, and why is its location so important anyway?"

Samantha pushed her point a step further. "I suspect you know where the captain's island is Maggie, and I suspect it's in the Caribbean. Right where my brother and that woman are stranded in a lifeboat. Your computer has told us that this captain is to be a part of Michael's immediate future. Am I getting warm?"

Maggie's nervousness became even more apparent. "All I know is what my computer has given us. The rest is all speculation."

"I don't think so," Samantha disagreed. "I think you know more than you're telling us. I think you know *exactly* where my brother is headed, and I think you're deliberately keeping me away from him. This isn't like you, Maggie. You've never kept things from me before."

Maggie was silent for a few moments. "All right, Sam," she finally gave in. "I should have known I couldn't keep you in the dark for long. I have been keeping some things from you but take my word for it, I've have my reasons."

"Reasons?" Samantha practically shouted. "What reasons? My brother is in trouble, Maggie. He needs me, and you won't let me go to him. Why?"

Maggie spoke quietly and calmly. "Believe me, Sam, if Michael needed you I'd be the first to send you to him. Trust me, everything is under control. You have my word, Michael is in no immediate danger."

"How can you say that, Maggie? Even if he's not in physical danger, he's still out there with that woman. If I don't get him away from her, he's going to be hurt again. I just know it."

"All right, Sam," Maggie yielded. "If you're that dead set on knowing the whole story, I'll tell you. But let me warn you, some of it is going to come as a shock."

"I'm a big girl, Maggie. Just tell me."

Maggie paused just long enough to take a deep breath, then came straight out with it. "Michael has a contract, Sam, like the one between you and Jason. The contract's between him and—"

Samantha's jaw dropped open. "No, Maggie! NOT—?"

"I'm afraid so, Sam. Michael and Jenice are contracted for each other. But being the high-spirited people they are, we're having a few problems getting them together."

Samantha fell back into the chair next to Maggie's desk. Her stomach was in knots. "I can't believe this, Maggie. My brother is contracted with Jenice Anderson? Are you sure about this? Couldn't there be some mistake?"

"There is no mistake, Sam. The contract is honored by the higher authorities. Do you want to argue with them?"

"Oh," Samantha groaned, laying her face in her hands. "I don't feel so good. BUT WAIT!" she cried, suddenly shooting out of her chair. "When Jason was courting me, I was told I had the right to choose Bruce over him if I wanted to. Does that same rule apply here? Can either Michael or Jenice choose to walk away from their contract?"

"I don't like the sound of what you're saying, Sam," Maggie cautioned. "It's not wise to play games with the higher authorities."

"But I am right, aren't I? Michael and Jenice do have the right to make up their own minds, don't they?"

"It is true, Sam. The higher authorities never force anyone into anything. But if you're contemplating enticing one or the other of them into something, I'd think twice if I were you. The higher authorities don't look kindly on that sort of meddling."

Looking Samantha straight in the eye, Maggie continued, "There's more to this story than I've told you so far, Sam. Not only is the contract between Michael and Jenice valid, but who do you think the higher authorities have appointed as the one responsible for getting them together?"

Samantha sat back down, her eyes widening. "Me?" she asked timidly.

"You," Maggie agreed.

"But . . . why would the higher authorities pick me?" Samantha sputtered. "They must know how I feel about Jenice. And how can anyone blame me for feeling like I do? Look at the way the woman hurt Bruce."

"Sam, you hurt Bruce, too—when you chose Jason over him."

"That's different. I did everything in my power to spare Bruce's feelings. You know that, Maggie. You helped me get Bruce and Arline together, remember?"

"Of course I remember, Sam. But Jenice did everything she could to spare Bruce's feelings, too. She asked him to do the trick with the parachute because she thought that was the easiest way to let him down."

"Parachute? Easiest way to let him down? Since when have you been one for puns, Maggie?" Samantha teased, then became deadly serious again. "But you're wrong about Jenice. She only challenged Bruce to jump out of a plane to make him look like a coward. She never thought Bruce would do it."

"You're judging her, Sam," Maggie reproved her. "The higher authorities don't like it when we judge. They reserve that right for themselves."

Samantha thought hard about what Maggie was saying. She had to admit, she was judging Jenice. But some people deserve to be judged, and Jenice was one of them. Not that Samantha wanted to argue with the higher authorities, but she didn't want to let Jenice off the hook, either. It felt good, disliking the woman. And no matter what anyone said about the matter, Jenice deserved it. Samantha turned to Maggie with another question.

"So that's why I couldn't get to the lifeboat with Michael and Jenice? And that's why you won't let me close to them now? You're afraid I'll do something to muddy the waters."

Maggie nodded. "That's the way it is, Sam. The higher authorities want you to pull them together, not drive them apart. You're an intricate part of the overall plan, but for the time being you have to give them some room. That's why I was worried when I thought you might have figured out that Michael and Jenice were headed for the island Captain Blake inhabits. I was having a hard enough time keeping you away from them as it was.

"There's a bit more, Sam. Michael and Jenice's contract is a big part of the plan, but they're not the only ones affected by it. There's much more at stake here than their contract alone. I'm limited on what I can tell you right now, but you'll understand soon enough. This much I guarantee."

As the meaning of Maggie's words became clear, Samantha was struck with another thought. "Michael's life never was in jeopardy, was it, Maggie? You only used that ploy to trick me into allowing Jenice in the picture, didn't you?"

Maggie laughed. "I give up, you've got that part figured out. In fact, it was my idea to put the question in the clouds to get you wondering how you and Jason would have met if destiny had gone according to plan. I knew you'd come straight to me for the answer, Sam. But, I wasn't lying to you. If Jason had been born when he was originally slated, he would have met Michael just like I said. It was scripted to happen in a supermarket where Michael was shopping. A magazine would have caught Michael's eye while he was standing in the checkout line, and he would have added the magazine to his other items. Then, as he was leaving the store, the magazine would have fallen unnoticed from his sack. At that point, destiny would have had

Jason retrieve the magazine and give it back to Michael. The two would have struck up a conversation, Michael would have suggested introducing Jason to his sister, and the rest would have been easy sailing."

"That's how I would have met Jason?" Samantha asked in surprise.

"That's it," Maggie positively affirmed.

Samantha slapped a hand to her forehead. "And the magazine would have been . . .?"

"*Life,* of course," Maggie laughed. "So you see, I wasn't lying— Jason really would have saved Michael's *Life.*"

"Oh brother," Sam groaned.

* * *

As Jenice told how she happened to be on the spot when the man in the ski mask pulled the gun, Michael hung on her every word.

"Crazy as it sounds, Michael, that's how it happened," she finished. "I was on the cruise ship because of George Glaser, my boss at the office. And I was there when the guy pulled the gun because of two angels, one of whom was your sister. Not that I could see her, but she was there, nevertheless. You can believe me, or you can call me a liar. But so help me, that's the way it happened, and there's nothing I can do to change the fact."

What Michael said next shocked her deeply. "I do believe you, Jenice," he said slowly. "I've heard about what happened on that beach that day. After Arline told me about Sam's death, she told me all about it. She didn't mention you by name, though, so I never suspected you were the other woman in Bruce's life."

"You say Arline *told* you about Sam's death?"

Michael rubbed the back of his neck. "Yeah. Let's just say I was out of touch with the family when Sam died. When I finally returned home, Arline was the first one I ran into. She and Bruce caught me by surprise at the airport. She learned that I was arriving from someone who worked for the airlines. I guess she had been trying to locate me through her television show for some time.

"They took me out to dinner, then to the resort they're running now. That was where Arline told me about Sam's death. Arline also told me how she met and talked to Samantha later. Knowing Sam was still out there somewhere, and that she was happy, did wonders to soften the blow of her death." He paused, a look of sorrow on his face. "Still, there was no excuse for my not being at her funeral."

Jenice was quiet for a moment, remembering. "That's right," she surmised. "You couldn't have been at Sam's funeral, could you? I would have seen you there."

"You were at the funeral?" Michael asked. "I don't understand. You didn't even know Sam."

"It's a long story, Michael. I was there because of my sister, who happens to be a friend of Bruce's. You wouldn't be interested in the details."

"Maybe not. But the fact is I wasn't there. And that's something I'll never forgive myself for." Unshed tears shone in Michael's eyes.

Jenice spoke softly. "If you don't mind my asking, how did you happen to be so far out of touch that your friends and family couldn't reach you with the news?"

Michael's eyes turned hard. "I was out of touch because I wanted it that way. I had some things I wanted to forget, and falling off the edge of the earth seemed like a good idea at the time."

Jenice had little trouble understanding Michael's meaning. *I'm so sorry, Michael,* she said in her own mind. *What I did was cruel. You didn't deserve to be hurt. Now I learn I'm responsible for you missing Sam's funeral as well. You have no idea what I'd give for the chance to live that day over again.*

But what would I have done differently? Would I really have given up my experience flying that Russian jet? I did my best to contact you by phone. And George certainly wasn't about to give me any more time. What would I have done differently? Heaven help me—what would I have done?

CHAPTER 8

How could a day starting out so perfectly end up entangled in such dilemma? From the beautiful green rolling hills of her childhood where she and Jason had stood this morning, to the cold depths of a valley named Jenice Anderson where she found herself now, Samantha just couldn't believe it. Jenice Anderson held a forever contract with her brother. And if that wasn't bad enough, she, Samantha Hackett, was the one chosen by the higher authorities to bring Jenice and Michael together. It wasn't fair.

Still, if a way around the problem could be found, it just might come more easily if Samantha was near the heart of the matter. Not that she would ever consider opposing the higher authorities, mind you. But, on the off chance either Jenice or Michael might choose to say "no" to the contract, how could anyone blame Samantha? And if she happened to stumble across a way to make a "no" from either of them inevitable, how could she be held responsible?

"All right, Maggie," she conceded. "I'll do it. But don't you think it would be better for me to get started right away? Shouldn't you get me to that lifeboat now?"

Maggie smiled one of those all-knowing smiles. "Let's not get ahead of ourselves," she suggested in a mild, but firm voice. "When the time comes I'll be the first to help you find Michael and Jenice. But for now, the plan doesn't include your being with them. Tell you what. I'll authorize you and Jason to use the viewing room. How's that?

"It's just down the hall and like the name implies, it's used for viewing certain events. We're set up for viewing almost anything, from past events to developments going on anywhere in the world at any given time. Naturally its use requires authorization from the higher authorities, but since I'm on the list I can do the authorizing. I'll zero in on Jenice and Michael. That way you can keep track of them even if you're not allowed to interfere just yet. I'll also program in a special introduction to Captain Blake, so you can get an idea of what he's like. You may find yourself working with the good captain, as well as Jenice and Michael, in the not too distant future."

"Tell me something, Maggie," Samantha asked wryly, "did you ever tune in on me when I was down there?"

"No, Sam," Maggie laughed. "You have my word. We never used the viewing room to spy on you. No need to. Jason kept a close vigil in your case."

Samantha had to admit, she wouldn't have liked having a viewing room used on her. And she didn't particularly like the idea of using one on her own brother. But given the choice between this, and trusting Michael alone with Jenice Anderson . . .

"Okay, Maggie. Take me to your viewing room. But if things start getting too serious between those two, you're going to hear from me."

* * *

Jenice pulled the blanket more tightly around herself to help shield her from the slight chill of the Caribbean night. Michael was at the other end of the lifeboat, doing much the same. Jenice wished things could be different. It would be so much nicer if the two of them could snuggle together under the same blanket. In her heart, Jenice longed to hold Michael, to kiss him, to whisper how much she had missed seeing him. In reality, this was impossible. She had long ago traded that option for a couple of rides in a Russian fighter jet.

"How did you happen to be on the cruise ship?" she asked, hoping to break some of the tension hanging over them like a dense fog.

"I won a contest," Michael replied. "But they failed to tell me the cruise included a night in a lifeboat when I claimed the tickets. How about you? You mentioned being here to cover a story, but you didn't say what the story was."

Jenice shrugged. "I wish I knew. George handed me the tickets and told me to be on the ship when it pulled out of the harbor. Crazy, huh?"

"So—you're a good reporter. Make the most of it. A firsthand account of being lost at sea should be pretty newsworthy, wouldn't you say?"

"That shows how much you know about news coverage," Jenice laughed. "If a great white cuts the boat in half and eats one or both of us, that's newsworthy. Floating around in the Caribbean? Forget it. Even a ho-hum documentary would upstage this."

Michael smiled and withdrew to his thoughts. A minute or so later, he approached a more personal subject. "This thing you had going with Bruce—how serious was it?"

The question caught Jenice cold. It was probably the last thing she expected to hear Michael ask. "I'll be honest, Michael. I met Bruce on the rebound. You said you had some forgetting to do? Well, believe it or not, so did I."

"Forgetting comes hard," Michael observed. "Some of us go about it in one way, and some in another. Me, I just wanted to be alone. You, apparently, wanted a pair of strong arms to help squeeze away your memories. Did you love him?"

"I've already told you I didn't love Bruce, although I admit I had feelings for him. He's a fine man. Arline is a very lucky woman to have him."

"You had feelings for Bruce? I suppose that's pretty evident from the way you let him down. At least he got a parachute and a wave good-bye."

Jenice brushed away a tear. "I guess I deserve that, Michael. You're right. I did at least show Bruce more courtesy than I showed you."

"Yeah, I guess. But we both ended up in the reject bin all the same. What's your problem, Jenice. Are you afraid of marriage?"

"Am I afraid of marriage?" Jenice said thoughtfully. "Who knows, maybe I am. Tell me, Michael, have you ever heard of Edmund Hillary and Tenzing Norgay?"

"Nope, can't say as I have. Who are they?"

"They're two men who made history on May 29, 1953, the same day my mother was born. They were the first to reach the summit of Mount Everest. It was always my mother's dream to follow in their footsteps, but she married my father instead. Don't get me wrong, I'm not putting my father down. He's a wonderful man, and my mother loves him dearly. But marrying him meant giving up her dream of exploring the world. I inherited that dream, Michael. Twice now, I've found myself faced with the same choice my mother had to make. First you asked me to marry you, then it was Bruce. Do you have any idea how hard it is for me to risk giving up my dream?"

Michael lay back and looked upward at the star-studded night sky. "Well, it makes little difference now, anyway. The ring I once offered you is somewhere in China, at the bottom of the Yangtze River. There's probably more chance of finding that ring than of ever finding what we lost that rainy afternoon at the Eiffel Tower."

"I'm sure you're right," Jenice agreed softly, then asked, "Would you like to know why I didn't keep our date at the Eiffel Tower?"

Michael lay back in the boat and pulled the blanket up to his neck. "No," he said flatly. "I really wouldn't. This may prove to be a long night. What do you say we try and get some sleep?"

An aching heart is a hard thing to put to rest. It was late into the night when Jenice finally drifted off to sleep.

* * *

It was the quiet hours of early morning now, and everyone on the island was asleep. Everyone, that is, except Captain Blake, who stood alone on the beach. The son of a seventeenth-century English fisherman, Blake had learned to love the sea as a small lad. He loved everything about the sea, right down to the smell of salt and dying seaweed. These were the sweetest perfumes to Blake's nostrils.

His one love other than the sea was Angela Marie. How he missed Angela's smiling face, a face he hadn't seen since that day three centuries ago, when they said good-bye on a foggy English morning.

"Must ye go?" Angela had pleaded, eyes filled with tears saltier than the ocean itself. "Ye know of me dreams about this voyage."

"It's me profession, Angela," Blake had argued. "Ye knew I be a sea captain when ye married me, woman."

"And ye knew about my special dreams when ye married me, Symington Blake. Ne'er have they been wrong, no, not even once. They be a warnin', that's what they be. This be a cursed voyage."

"Nonsense, woman. This be a voyage that will bring us a pretty price. A pretty price, my fair Angela, for Oscar Welborn be a wealthy man. And old Oscar be promisin' ta make me a wealthy man if I deliver the lady to her destination. 'Tis me last voyage, Angela. Ye have me word on it. And me word . . ."

"I know what yer word be, Captain Blake. But I know what my dreams be, too. If ye board that ship, I give ye MY word—ye'll not be comin' home to me this time."

Captain Blake's heart ached as he recalled Angela's prophetic words. "Aye, lassie, and if I'd only listened to ye, I would not be standin' alone on this forsaken beach tonight. I'd be somewhere up there past those shiny stars, cradled in yer warm, lovin' arms. Brad Douglas be right about me, ye know. He says I be a stubborn one all right. But I've given me word, and me word is me bond."

The good captain must have stood on this same beach, having this same conversation with himself, a thousand times, over the past centuries. Even though he didn't know it, one thing was different about this early morning from all the others. This time he wasn't alone. This time there were two more angels watching, and listening, in a viewing room from another dimension.

CHAPTER 9

Jenice shivered. It was cold, extremely cold. But what else could she expect with all that snow? As far as the eye could see, in any direction, the ground was blanketed with a thick coat of frozen snow. Jenice was glad for the parka and hood that protected every inch of her, except for one small patch around her eyes. Only one slope was left to be mastered, and Mount Everest would be hers. She would stand at the top of the world looking out over a conquered dream. A dream carried in her heart since the days of her childhood.

Strange—she would never have expected to hear the sound of breaking waves. Not here, deep in the Himalayas. Suddenly her eyes opened wide. There was no parka, only the cotton blanket. The snow was gone. Instead, she found herself staring at the inside hull of a lifeboat.

"Breaking waves!" she called out abruptly as reality came into focus. "That could only mean . . ." In an instant she had the blanket off and was up staring at . . .

"LAND! Michael, we've found land!"

Michael's response was cool and assured. "I know. Whatever force had control of the lifeboat brought us here during the night."

Blinking the sleep from her eyes, Jenice realized Michael was at the oars pulling the boat toward what appeared to be a small, densely vegetated island. A glance upward revealed the first streamers of a huge red sun, just penetrating the blackness in the eastern sky.

"Where are we, Michael?" she asked. "What island is it?"

Michael shrugged and shook his head. "Don't know for sure. Could be any one of dozens. The Caribbean is full of small islands, some uninhabited." He released a loud sigh. "I suspect this one may be uninhabited. It's a small one, all right. And so far there's no sign of life."

"Oh great. First we spend the night drifting around in a lifeboat. Now we find ourselves playing *Gilligan's Island*. We don't even have the skipper with us." Jenice took a closer look. "What do you figure, Michael? Is it safe?"

Michael laughed. "I don't think we're going to run into Big Foot, if that's what you have in mind."

"Big Foot," she said, joining in with his laughter. "Funny you should mention Big Foot. I was just dreaming about where he's supposed to live, in the Himalayas. I think the Caribbean might be a bit warm for him, at that. That doesn't mean there might not be other dangers on this island. Snakes maybe, or quicksand. If the place is uninhabited, there's probably a reason."

"There you go, thinking like a reporter again. There can't be anything bad enough on the island to risk staying in this lifeboat under a blistering sun. And besides, we were brought here by 'the force.' Who knows what could happen if we oppose it? We might end up doing battle with Darth Vader. I don't know about you, Jenice, but my cruise ticket didn't come with one of those flashlight sword things we'd need to fight good old Darth."

"Very funny, Michael Allen. You don't know for sure we were brought here by some sort of force. Just because you couldn't turn the boat around last night . . ."

"There's more to it than just trying to turn the boat, Jenice. All night long I tried the oars. Whatever was holding us refused to let go 'til we came in sight of this island. I can't explain it, but I'd stake my life on the fact that we were brought here for a reason."

"'Lifeboat Dragged Ruthlessly across Caribbean Sea by Strange Unexplainable Force Which Refuses to Stop until It Deposits Its Occupants on Uninhabitable Island in the Middle of Nowhere!'" Jenice laughed. "You know what, Michael? I think I'd have a little trouble selling that one to old George."

"I don't know about your editor, but I do know there's no such place as the middle of nowhere. We're somewhere in the Virgin Islands, probably not far from Saint Thomas. I figure if we build a signal fire, the smoke may attract the attention of a passing ship, or maybe a plane."

"Or maybe someone on Saint Thomas Island itself," Jenice suggested. "If it is close enough, that is. Good idea, Michael. I vote we put ashore and build ourselves a fire."

Michael stopped rowing and leaned forward, resting for a moment on the oars. "We're bound to be missed by now. Back on *The Wandering Star*, I mean. That is, if that actor fellow told them about us."

"That is, *if* he told someone about us. I don't know how far that guy can be trusted. If he decided to ignore us, it could be hours, maybe days, before we're missed. You know what I find strange in all this, Michael? All my life I've wanted to visit a deserted island. Now it looks like I may get my chance, and all I can think of is being rescued. Crazy, huh?"

Michael starting rowing again. "Maybe not so crazy. You might feel differently if you were in this boat with someone besides me. I'm sure you can't wait to get clear of my company."

Taking a deep breath, Jenice looked up at the brilliant morning sky. "Listen, Michael," she said. "You and I had one wonderful summer together. Maybe, if I had been more willing to toss aside some of my dreams, we might have had much more. But I wasn't and I didn't. I hurt you and I'm sorry."

Lowering her eyes she looked straight at Michael. "Now we find ourselves thrown together under the strangest of circumstances, like it was all planned by someone bigger than either of us. It's not my fault we're here and it's not your fault. What do you say we let yesterday bury its mistakes and let's make the best of a bad situation. How bad can it be? A few days, at the worst, a week out of our lives. Then it'll be all over. You can go your way and I'll go mine. With luck, our paths will never cross again. I vote we forget what might have been and just pretend we're a couple of strangers caught up in this weird adventure. Deal?"

Jenice went on with her self-constructed lie. It seemed the best way, at the moment at least, to shield her true feelings of guilt and pain. "I'm sure, Michael. It's best for both of us, believe me."

Michael's expression turned to stone. "What you're asking isn't easy, Jenice. I find thinking of you as a stranger a little difficult. But— if you're sure that's what you want . . ."

"I'm sure, Michael. It's best for both of us, believe me."

Michael swallowed hard. "Yeah," he agreed. "You're probably right. I'll give it my best shot."

"Michael, look!" Jenice suddenly shouted, pointing toward the beach where they were headed. "The island's not deserted after all. There's a man, on the beach there."

Michael glanced over his shoulder. "You're right. Where did he come from? He wasn't there last time I looked."

Jenice strained to get a better look. "Talk about weird. This guy looks like he just stepped out of the pages of some pirate novel. You don't suppose we've happened onto Treasure Island by chance?"

"He does look a little out of place," Michael agreed. "Maybe he's an actor. We might have stumbled onto a movie set here. That could be good."

"What, you think we might be discovered? They probably already have Mel Gibson and Meg Ryan cast as the leads. What chance would we have landing parts, even if they are making a movie?"

"You know what I mean, Jenice. Movie people would have communication to the outside world. Maybe even transportation. Wait! Now the guy's gone. How could he have vanished so fast? I hardly took my eyes off him."

"You're right, he is gone. What sort of man could—hey! You don't suppose that could have been Jason, do you? With a pirate costume, I mean. That would explain how he could appear and vanish so fast. Speaking of his vanishing, he sure pulled a quick exit when we ended up in this lifeboat."

Michael peered at the place where the man in costume had been standing. "I don't think so, Jenice. This guy I could see; your Jason I couldn't."

"True," Jenice said. "Maybe this guy's so fast because he's a track star training for the Olympics."

"A track star? Dressed in a pirate costume? Give me a break, Jenice."

"I said 'maybe', didn't I?"

* * *

Brad rubbed his eyes and stared at the figure standing near the foot of his bed. "What in blazes is wrong with you, Blake? Can't a man sleep in peace?"

"I be interruptin' your sleep, Brad Douglas, for a very good cause indeed. 'Tis intruders we have on this here island. If ye'd be so kind as to be gettin' yer clothes on, I'll take ye to where they be landing this very minute. And I'd be greatly appreciative if ye'd be quick about it. I don't want these meddlin' souls stumblin' onto somethin' that be none of their business."

Brad sat up in bed, suddenly wide awake. "We have visitors on the island?" he exclaimed. "Who, for crying out loud? No one ever comes here."

"A man and a woman, says I. They be in a longboat, just off the western shore. By thunder, they be up to no good, matey. I feel it in me bones."

"You don't have any bones, Blake. Other than those lying out there in that hidden cave you're so protective of. Just because someone's paying us a visit doesn't mean they're up to no good."

"I have me ghostly bones, and they be tellin' me these folks are up to no good. Slip on them trousers and let's have ourselves a look."

Brad was out of bed and dressed in a matter of seconds. Having visitors to the island was an oddity, and he was nearly as anxious to learn who they were, and the nature of their business, as Blake was. Grabbing his old straw hat from the post atop his dresser, Brad glanced in the mirror. For the most part, he avoided mirrors these days. He hated seeing the evidence of what he had become during these many years outside of civilization. His hair was long and unruly, as was his full facial beard. If anything, his beard was even fuller than Captain Blake's, though the color was greatly different. Brad's beard was red, while the captain's was jet black. If Lori could see him now . . . She'd never believe a man who had spent so much time and effort molding Hollywood actors into glamorous stars could ever let himself go like this. Sometimes, Brad couldn't believe it himself. Where he was and what he was doing now was a far cry from the days he directed motion pictures for the infamous Howard Placard. Sometimes Brad missed the fun and action of being a director, but those days were gone forever. Howard Placard had vowed that Brad would never work in the industry again, and when Howard set out to blacklist someone—that someone was blacklisted forever. But all that was about another place and another time. Right now Brad had the pressing matter of visitors on the island to be handled.

Leaving the house as quietly as possible, so as not to awaken the others, Brad followed the old sea captain along the trail leading to the western beach. It was a typically beautiful morning. A light ground fog added a dampness to the air that intensified every little sound. Songs from a few early birds could be heard on all sides, while the occasional cracking of a dead branch under Brad's heavy boots announced to the whole island that someone was on the move. Soon Brad and Captain Blake reached the edge of the rain forest and stepped onto the sandy beach just in time to see the two occupants of the lifeboat dragging it ashore.

"Yo there!" Brad called out, waving his hand as he walked. "Are you folks in need of help?"

* * *

Jenice glanced up at the sound of a male voice. The first person coming into view was the pirate fellow, the one they had seen from the lifeboat. And this time he had company. "They look friendly enough to me," she whispered to Michael. "What do you think?"

"I think we play it by ear," he said softly. "What choice do we have?"

Michael dropped the line he was holding and extended his hand as the two men drew near. "Hi," he said. "I'm Michael Allen and this is Jenice Anderson. And to answer your question, yes, we could use some help. We've managed to get ourselves in a bit of a pickle, it seems."

"A bit of a pickle, eh?" Brad responded, accepting Michael's hand. "Doesn't surprise me. What would surprise me is hearing you say you came to this island for a little R & R. I'm Brad Douglas."

After shaking hands with Michael, Brad extended his hand to Jenice. "Glad to make your acquaintance, too, ma'am," he said.

Jenice accepted his hand. "Likewise, Brad. But what about your friend here, aren't you going to introduce him?"

Brad and the captain exchanged surprised glances. "You can see my friend?" Brad gasped. "I—I don't get it."

"You don't get it?" Jenice was confused. "I don't get it either. Why wouldn't I see him? He's standing right in front of me."

Brad was visibly stunned. "What about you?" he asked Michael. "Can you see the captain, too?"

Michael nodded. "Yeah, I see him. Is there something wrong with that?"

Brad's eyes moved rapidly back and forth between the captain, and the two visitors. "Yes," he affirmed. "There is something wrong. I'm just not sure what. All I know is you're the only ones ever to see the captain—other than me, that is. This isn't easy to explain, but . . ."

Like pieces of a jigsaw puzzle, little bits and sections started coming together in Jenice's mind. Jason Hackett for instance. And the unseen force pushing her and Michael into the lifeboat. "Let me make a stab, here," she said to Brad. "The captain, as you call him, isn't a man, is he? He's . . ."

"A ghost," Brad blurted out.

Jenice looked first at the captain, and then to Brad. "I was about to use the word 'angel'," she said.

"Angel? Ha! I'd never refer to Blake as an angel. He's a ghost, all right. But no one else has ever seen him before. I just don't get it."

"I don't get it, either," Michael confessed. "But several things have happen lately that I don't understand. Jenice here is an old hand at talking with angels, or ghosts if you prefer. Me—well—this is a first."

"You really are a ghost?" Jenice asked calmly.

"Aye, lassie, I be a ghost. Are ye not afraid of me?"

"Afraid of you? No, should I be?"

Blake straightened with indignation. "By thunder, ye be a sassy one, says I. I'd be obliged if ye would state yer business here on me island. I don't take lightly to visitors on me shores."

Jenice remained unshaken. "Brad called you Blake. That is your name, I presume."

"Aye, that be me name. Captain Horatio Symington Blake to be exact. And I make no bones about not wantin' ye on me island."

"Fine, Captain Blake. If you or your friend here will just get me to a phone where I can call for some help, I'll be gone faster than you can tune your harp—or wash your sheet—whatever."

Blake ran his fingers through his beard. "Ye have a bit of the dragon's fire in your tongue, lassie," he declared. "Ye remind me of me own Angela Marie."

Brad laughed. "I have no idea why she can see you, Blake. But the lady obviously has your number, my friend."

Brad turned his attention to Jenice. "You have to understand—Captain Blake here thinks he holds a monopoly on this island. He's been guarding it for the last three hundred years."

"Three hundred years?" Jenice gasped.

"Oh yes. And don't feel like he's singled you out for a hard time. You should have seen the way he acted when I first arrived. Fortunately, his boo is worse than his fright. You say you need to use a phone. What exactly is the problem?"

"The problem is," Jenice explained, "we managed to get ourselves stranded in that lifeboat over there. We were on a cruise ship and—well it's a long story. But here we are on your island. And we need help. I'd hoped they would have missed us by now. Have you heard any news yet this morning?"

"We don't get much news here, I'm afraid. Just what I receive on my shortwave radio. I haven't had that fired up since yesterday afternoon. How long you been floating around out there anyway?"

"All night," Jenice answered.

"All night, eh? You must be pretty hungry by this time. My place is about five minutes from here. How 'bout I fix up some breakfast and we can take up this conversation from there?"

"Ye be fixin' their breakfast, will ye?" Blake scoffed. "I'll have no part of these castaway intruders snoopin' around me island, Brad Douglas. If ye refuse to put them back afloat in that there longboat, then ye might at least be findin' some way of gettin' them off me island."

"Pay no mind to him," Brad sighed. "My offer of breakfast stands, if you're hungry."

In all the excitement, Jenice hadn't thought about food. But at the mention of breakfast, she suddenly realized just how hungry she really was. Thanks to Jason's untimely interruption, she had missed dinner last night. "Breakfast sounds great to me," she quickly said.

"Sounds good to me, too," Michael agreed.

"I'll be havin' no part of this!" Blake grumbled again. Throwing both hands high over his head, he stormed off into the thickness of the rain forest.

"Let him go," Brad laughed. "He'll get over it." Then, pointing a thumb toward the trail he had emerged from earlier, he said, "This way, follow me. We'll get you fed, then we'll talk about getting you rescued."

* * *

In the viewing room, Samantha was fuming as she sat helplessly beside Jason and watched the events as they unfolded.

"I'm telling you, Jason, I don't like this one bit. All I can do is sit here and watch. It's just not fair; Michael needs my help. Especially since that woman is with him."

"Now Sam, you remember what Maggie told you about Jenice and Michael. You'll just have to work on changing your attitude."

"You don't need to remind me, smarty. I remember what she said."

"Right down to the part about your being responsible for getting the two of them together?"

"I remember it all, Jason Hackett. But I don't like it. And I don't like learning that my brother already spent a whole summer romantically linked to that hussy. You saw what she did to him, didn't you. If I'm anything, Jason, I'm a great judge of character. I'm telling you, Jenice has no character. She's already hurt my brother once, and she'll do it again if she's given the chance."

"Sam! Didn't you hear a word Maggie said? Giving her a second chance is exactly what you're supposed to do. And don't try telling me you don't know how to play Cupid. I saw the way you finagled things around to get Bruce and Arline together."

Samantha had a few more things she thought needed to be said, but she bit her tongue and looked back at the scene unfolding before them on the holographically enhanced display screen.

"Did you see anything strange about what just went on at that beach?" she asked.

"I saw the same thing you did. What are you getting at, Sam?"

"I'm getting to the point of Michael and Jenice seeing Captain Blake. That doesn't fit the ordinary rules, and you know it."

Jason scratched the back of his head. "Yeah, you got a point there, Sam. Offhand, I'd say the higher authorities have pretty much thrown the rule book away on this case. There must be something pretty special about this one."

"There is something special about this case," Maggie broke in. She had slipped into the viewing room, unnoticed by either Jason or Samantha. "Several things, in fact. Like it or not, the two of you are set to play big parts in the whole scenario."

"Meaning hooking my brother up with Jenice Anderson." Samantha suggested sarcastically.

"That, and more," Maggie avowed. "I want you to think about something, Sam. When you took on the assignment to bring Arline and Bruce together, did you enjoy it?"

Samantha didn't even have to think before answering this question. "Sure I enjoyed it, Maggie. It was great fun, and it turned out perfect in the end. Why do you ask?"

"I have my reasons, Sam. What about your assignment with your cousins Lisa and Julie? Did you enjoy working with them?"

Samantha smiled. "You're darn right I did. Especially locking horns with Uncle Mac. I guess I showed him a thing or two, didn't I?"

"The case I'm making is, you seem to enjoy an occasional assignment like these. Am I right? You've even said you'd like to have more assignments, haven't you?"

"Yeah, I have. Who knows, maybe it's because my own life on the other side was cut short. But I still don't get your point, Maggie."

"My point is, the higher authorities very often hold us to our words. You said you wanted more assignments, and the higher authorities took you literally."

"Uh oh," Samantha moaned. "That's how I ended up being assigned to play Cupid with Michael and Jenice, isn't it?"

"By your own words, Sam," Maggie confirmed.

"That's not fair, Maggie. This thing with Jenice and Michael is not the sort of assignment I had in mind."

"Ah—but when it comes to dealing with the higher authorities, we don't get to pick and choose what they offer. You said you wanted more assignments, and that's exactly what you've been given. And you might as well know now, your assignment extends beyond Jenice and your brother. You, Sam, have been chosen to straighten out a couple more big problems while you're at it. For one thing, it's your chore to get the illustrious Captain Blake off the middle of the fence and over to this side of forever where he belongs."

"I what?!" Samantha gasped.

"You heard me, Sam. The higher authorities have made Captain Blake part of your assignment. I'm sure you'll have great fun with that one. And when you're finished with Blake, you get to handle the little problem our friend Brad faces because he lost the one love of his life."

"The woman of his life?" Samantha guessed. "The one he calls Lori, you mean?"

"One and the same, lady."

Samantha lay a hand to her forehead. "Oh my," she said. "It looks like my mouth has gotten me into a good one this time. I'm supposed to convince my brother he's in love with a woman I dislike immensely, find a way to get a stubborn three-hundred-year-overdue ghost to his side of the line, and fix whatever's wrong with Brad and his Lori all in one fell swoop? Wonderful. Just wonderful, Maggie."

Maggie laughed. "Sort of makes you want to watch what you say more closely in the future, doesn't it? But to put your mind a little at ease, you'll have time for a breather before having to tackle the problem of Brad and Lori. At least a month, maybe two."

* * *

"Umm, this bacon is scrumptious," Jenice said. "And these eggs are so fresh. If you don't mind my asking, where do you do your shopping? Are there stores on this island?"

"Do we have stores?" Brad laughed. "Not hardly. I did all the shopping for breakfast right in my own back yard."

Jenice looked at Brad. "And by that you mean . . . ?"

"I mean, I raise my own groceries. I have chickens, and I always keep a pig or two around for when I want to play Jimmy Dean. I even have a milk cow. Living on an island sometimes takes a little ingenuity."

"You raise everything yourself?" Jenice asked in amazement. "How many people live on this island, anyway?"

Brad took a drink of guava juice and set his glass on the table. "Well that all depends on whether or not you count my friend the ghost. With him included, there are four of us."

Jenice's mouth dropped open. "Only four people on this whole island?"

"That's three people and one ghost," Brad corrected. "Once you get a feel for just how small this island is, four will sound like a crowd, I assure you."

"An island with a population of four," Jenice mused aloud. "I've always dreamed of visiting this kind of place. I hope we have time to look it over before our rescuers get here."

"Time doesn't mean much on our island, Jenice. So as far as I'm concerned, you can spend as much time as you like before we figure out how to get you back to your cruise ship. I'm sure the girls will agree. We don't get much company you know."

"Girls?" Jenice asked.

"My sister, Shannon, and niece, Tanielle. They make up the other half of the population. They should be dragging in any time now. Especially when they smell breakfast."

"That's it? Just you, your sister, and your niece? I take it this is the only house on the island."

"Yep. There's just this one."

"From the looks of the place," Jenice said, looking around, "I'd say your ingenuity goes a little further than just growing breakfast. This place would look great on any street in the good old USA. Did you build it yourself?"

"Every nail and board," Brad smiled.

"Wow! I'll bet it cost you a bundle."

"Not really. Like everything else I do here, I built it on the barter system with the folks on Saint Thomas and Saint John Islands."

"Barter system?" Jenice was fascinated. "Let me guess—you do construction work for them, and they give you the materials you need to build your house, and the like."

"I do some construction work," Brad explained. "But mostly I entertain."

Jenice had noticed a piano as they passed through the living room on their way to the kitchen. "You're an entertainer? Let me guess. You play the piano?"

"The piano is part of my act," Brad answered modestly. "I play it as a background for my act. I'm an impressionist and a darn good one if I do say so myself. I do requests from my audience. I can mimic the rich and famous, or I can do the poor and unheard of. Wanna hear my version of Walt Riley?"

"Who's Walt Riley?" Jenice asked.

"Walt's a meat cutter I once met in Des Moines, Iowa."

Jenice squinted at Brad. "Walt Riley, eh? Who else can you impersonate? Preferably someone I might know."

"Well, Leann Rimes is a little out of my category. How about you pick someone?

"Okay, let's stick to one of the old standbys. How about John Wayne?"

"John Wayne? Well now, let me tell ya', little lady—I can do John Wayne just about as good as any man alive. Ta tell ya the truth—I can probably do John Wayne better than John Wayne could do himself. And I can do it without the horse."

"All right," Jenice laughed. "You got the Duke down for sure. You are good, Brad. I'll bet your audiences love you."

"I don't know if they love me—but they like me well enough to keep inviting me back. And that's how I've managed to make life a little more comfortable for the three of us living on this island."

Michael spoke up. "Something I noticed is your electricity and running water. I'm curious. How do you manage it?"

"It's a snap," Brad said. "You've never seen rain like we get here. I trap rain water in a tank on a hill out back of the house. My power comes from batteries and a wind-driven generator."

"I'm impressed," Michael acknowledged. "How about a phone? You got one of those?"

"Nope. I haven't owned a phone for the past ten years. Got the next best thing to it, though."

"Your shortwave radio?"

"Bingo. I assume you're pressing me to get your rescue underway."

Jenice glanced over at Michael, and for a brief instant their eyes met. In that instant she had a driving urge to tell him no. *Forget about being rescued. Let's stay right here on this little island awhile and see what we can do about taking up where Paris left off.* Her thoughts were cut off abruptly at the sight of a very lovely woman entering the kitchen.

"Well, would you look at this," the lady said with a certain cheeriness in her voice. "We not only have company, but my brother has actually fixed breakfast. Talk about good things coming in packages of two. Hi, I'm Shannon—Brad's sister—in case he hasn't told you."

"Ah, good morning, sis. This is Jenice Anderson and Michael Allen. They got themselves in a little bit of a bad situation and drifted up on our shore in a lifeboat."

"In a lifeboat? Nothing serious, I hope?"

"Not really," Jenice volunteered. "We just managed to get ourselves separated from our cruise ship. I'm sure with your brother's help we can join the others with little harm done. I'm happy to meet you, Shannon."

Shannon eyed the breakfast spread. "I see you have a couple of extra places set," she said. "Is one of them mine, by chance, big brother?"

Brad smiled and swished his hand toward an empty chair. "Be my guest, sis."

"I think I will," Shannon grinned. "This looks pretty good. It's nice to eat someone else's cooking once in awhile."

"How about me, Uncle Brad," a sleepy-eyed, fifteen-year-old said, as she staggered into the kitchen in her bathrobe. "Your hot cakes smell so good I couldn't sleep any more. Where's mine?"

* * *

As the little group enjoyed breakfast and getting acquainted, another scene was unfolding a mile or so offshore from the island. A small motorboat, with a lone occupant at the controls, sped toward the island at full throttle. Deliberately choosing a small cove where the boat could be kept out of sight, the driver docked. Slipping into the thick rain forest, he proceeded to make his way toward a water tower that could be seen a little above the terrain.

CHAPTER 10

Samantha stared at Maggie. "All right, I agree I can't work with Michael and Jenice until the higher authorities give me a green light, but if I'm responsible for Captain Blake I'd really like to get started with him. Trust me, Maggie. Tell me where the island is, and I promise to stay clear of my brother. I'll meet with the captain, and be about my business. Okay?"

Maggie gave the offer some serious thought. "Can you really be that close to Michael and not go to him, Sam?"

"I can do it, Maggie. I won't like it, but I can do it. I'd just like to get a feel for what I'm up against with Captain Blake."

"How about you, Jason?" Maggie asked. "Do you want to go with Sam to see the captain?"

Jason quickly shook off the idea. "I need to check in at the Paradise Palace, Maggie. As the head chef, I have to stay on top of things. Sam doesn't need me to help out with the captain. Knowing her, she'll have the wind in his homebound sails faster than he can count the letters in his name."

"Make that the letters in his last name," Samantha laughed. "How about it, Maggie? You want to point out the location of that island?"

* * *

Finding the island with Maggie's direction was a snap. Finding Blake wasn't that much harder. He was in a clearing near the center of the island. Samantha came up from behind to watch him at the edge of the clearing, where he stared into the darkness of a partially obscured cave.

The idea of coercing this stubborn ghost into giving up his ridiculous island vigil wasn't something she particular relished, but since the higher authorities had given her the job she thought it best to dive right in.

"Morning, Captain Blake," she said, catching him off guard. "Nice cave. Is this where your bones lie?"

The captain spun around to face her and nearly lost his balance. "Blast ye, woman!" he growled. "Who be ye, and by what right do ye come sneakin' up on me poor soul in such a manner?"

"Name's Samantha. And I wasn't sneaking up on you. You were so engrossed in your own little world you just didn't notice me."

"By the stars, this can't be happening! Ye be the third intruder to me island in one day. And the third to see me face while yer about it." Blake's left eye squinted nearly closed. "Who be ye, woman? And what be yer business on me island?"

"I already told you, I'm Samantha. And I'm here to talk some sense into that three-hundred-year-old skull of yours."

Blake took a closer look. "Unless I miss me guess, ye be a ghost like me, lassie. Be it so?"

"Ghost, angel, call me what you like. But don't say I'm like you, buster. I had the good sense to cross the line into the other dimension when my time came."

Blake eyed the cave entrance nervously, then stepped quickly away from it. "I ask ye, lassie, why be ye here in place of Gus? He be the one obliged to look in on me now and again."

Samantha gave a halfhearted laugh. "Believe me, I'd just as soon they had sent Gus. I'd sure like to know where Gus is about now. I suspect he has a lot more to do with what's going on here than Maggie's owning up to. If I'm right, he and I are in for a few words before this is over."

Samantha moved toward the cave entrance. "This is interesting," she said. "Is this part of the big secret you're so afraid someone will stumble onto?"

"Get away from me cave!" Blake cried out, rushing to block her from getting too close. "What's in there be none of yer business, lassie."

"That's where you're wrong, Blake," she said, brushing him aside and peering into the darkness of the cave. "Everything about you is my business now. The higher authorities have decided it's time you came over to the other side where you belong, so they're sending in the heavy troops—me. You might as well get packed, fella. You've met your match this time, and you're about to make a long overdue trip home."

Blake's chin shot forward as he folded both arms across his chest. "By the stars, woman, I'll not budge an inch. Not 'til I keeps me word to the blood kin of Oscar Welborn."

"Yeah, well if that's the case—then you'd better be filling me in on exactly what it is you want to give to this Welborn's offspring. I want to hear your story, Blake. The whole story, and I want to hear it now. I might not be able to force you across the line, but I can make life pretty miserable for you if you don't. All it takes is one word from me and you, Mister Horatio Symington Blake, are banished from this island forever. If you insist on staying on this side, then you can figure on spending your time smack dab in the middle of the Sahara Desert. So how do you like them oysters, pal?"

Blake's eyes shot open. "Ye be wantin' ta send me to a desert?! Over me dead body, woman!"

Samantha was unperturbed. "That's okay, too. I can arrange to have your bones moved along with you, if that's the way you want it."

"I'll not listen to one more word of this nonsense! Captain Blake is a seaman, and a seaman he'll remain. I'd sooner rot in the king's dungeon than spend me time on a desert."

"Sorry, Blake. The king's dungeon is not an option. Now unless you're ready to start looking at a lot of camels, you better start moving your tongue fast. I want your whole story, and I want it now."

Blake removed his hat and nervously ran his fingers through his thick crop of hair. "Ye means business, don't ye, lassie. Ye really do have the power to move me to the Sahara Desert."

"I do and I will if you don't cooperate with me."

Blake replaced the hat and stared hard at Samantha. "Ye be bluffin', says I. That be me gut feelin'."

Samantha's face twisted into a catlike grin. "Bluffing, am I? Well, there's one way to find out. I'm giving you just one minute, Blake."

"Woman, yer heart is colder than the wind over me sails on a Christmas day in the Greenland Sea."

"So I've been told. Whatever it takes, my friend."

"Me whole life is the sea. This be embarrassin', lassie. I'm glad me mateys aren't here to see Captain Horatio Symington Blake on the plank by the sword of a woman. Aye, but it's me white flag I'll be raisin' to ye. I'll tell ye me story, but only after ye give me yer word of secrecy. I'd be obliged for yer promise to tell no man—or woman—the things yer about to hear."

"I'll go you one better, Blake. I not only give you my word not to reveal your secret before you're ready for me to, I also promise to do everything in my power to help you find a descendant of this Oscar Welborn. I want you on the other side where you belong, but that doesn't mean closing my eyes to your dilemma. I have no doubt I can find the person you're looking for, considering the advanced technology I have at my disposal. You cooperate with me, and I think I can guarantee we'll both get what we're after. For starters, you can tell me if this cave is where your bones are resting."

"Aye, lassie," Blake sighed. "As me ship was slippin' away ta meet Davie Jones, I managed ta salvage one of the long boats off her deck. Bein' the expert navigator I am, I had little trouble findin' me way to this here island. At the time I figured to stay on here just long enough for some wanderin' sailor to come within me sight. A good plan it was, too, lassie. There be plenty of everything a man needs to survive right here on this rock in the middle of the ocean. And this here cave proved to be all the shelter this old captain needed from the chill of the rain and winds blowin' off the waves of the deep. Aye, I was doin' fine until I decided to go explorin' deeper into the black bowels of me cave. How was I to know that cursed rock would send me tumblin' into a hole that dropped to the belly of the earth? But, says I, that's just the way it happened. And now me bones lie at the bottom of this miserable pit, lassie. This cave be me tomb.

"And me witherin' bones be not the only thing that lie on the floor of this blackened pit. Clutched in me boney fingers be a leather pouch containin' the map that I promised to get into the hands of Oscar Welborn's descendant. The map be the reason this here cave has remained me secret all these years. It be my responsibility to see this map never falls in the wrong hands. That, says I, would be a fate worse than a thousand lashings at the hand of the king's keeper of the tortures."

"Uh huh," Samantha said with a nod of her head. "And the map, I assume, shows the location of your sunken ship?"

"Aye, lassie. That be what the map shows."

"Okay, Blake. That about brings us down to the nitty gritty. I think you know what I mean, don't you?"

Blake's head lowered until he was looking at the ground near his feet. "Ye be askin' me to tell the final secret. Ye wants to know about the lady."

Samantha folded her arms and grinned widely. "You got it, friend. That's exactly what I want to hear. Go ahead, make my day."

* * *

Jenice watched as Brad powered up his shortwave radio. A turmoil of emotion ran through her mind as she realized their rescuers were only as far away as his microphone. If only there was a way to postpone their rescue a little longer. This tiny island offered an adventure almost beyond words. So much lay out there just waiting for her to explore. And these people were fantastic. Brad, his sister, Shannon, and Tanielle—they were all so friendly and fun to be with. A smile crossed her lips as she thought how even the island's resident ghost added his special air to the place. Oh sure, he acted gruff, but Jenice had him pegged as a soft-hearted, colorful character under the mask he wore for appearance's sake.

Though she had a hard time admitting it, there was one paramount reason she wished their rescue could be put on hold, for a while at least. Maybe, just maybe she and Michael—but no, that was something never to be. All the arguments her mind could conjure up wouldn't change the fact that a speedy return to their normal lives was the best possible—the only possible—answer.

"I don't understand this," Brad said after several minutes turning dials on his radio. "I've never had trouble with this rig before."

"What's the problem?" Michael asked. "The radio has to be working. I can hear conversations as you change channels."

"You can hear conversations," Brad explained. "The problem is, I can't talk back to them. My transmitter is deader than my friend the captain. I can't get out on this thing at all."

Hearing mention of the captain brought a question from Jenice. "I notice you never mentioned your friend the captain around your sister or Tanielle," she said. "Are either of them even aware of your relationship with a ghost?"

Shannon and her daughter had offered to clean up after breakfast so that Brad and the others could retire to his radio room to make the call for outside help. This meant they were out of earshot at the moment, leaving Jenice free to voice her question.

"Do you think I'm crazy!" Brad laughed. "I have a hard enough time believing *I* talk to a ghost myself, let alone trying to explain it to them. Which brings us back to the point of you and Michael seeing Blake. No one but me has ever seen him before. And that's another thing I can't explain."

"Our seeing Blake is not the only unexplainable thing that's been happening to the two of us lately," Michael explained. "Case in point, your radio. The only time it refuses to work is when you attempt to use it for our sakes."

"Yeah, well, be that as it may," Brad came back, shaking off Michael's peculiar suggestion. "This radio is not my only means of getting you some help. I still have my boat. We're not that far from Saint Thomas Island."

"A boat?" Michael asked anxiously. "One with a motor, I hope. I've had about all the fun I can stand pulling on a set of oars."

"Oh yes," Brad laughed. "My boat has a motor. It runs great, too. Unless the little gremlins that are following you around have messed with that too."

"Not funny," Michael grimaced. "Not after all that's happened to us so far. Don't even joke about having trouble with your boat."

"You're going to the main island?" Tanielle asked excitedly as Brad and the others returned to the kitchen with their story.

"Yep, honey. Wanna go along?"

"Can I Mom?" Tanielle asked, more excited than ever.

"Are you sure she won't be in the way?" Shannon asked.

"In the way? I'd love to have her company, sis. You should know that. You're welcome to come along, too, if you like. There's plenty of room in the boat."

"Really, Brad, I'd rather stay here and catch up on some late writing. My publisher is pushing for the final manuscript in less than a week. Tanielle can go along, if you're sure it's all right."

"You're a writer?" Jenice asked.

Shannon nodded yes. "I write novels. It's something I love, and it helps keep my sanity here on this isolated island."

"How neat! I do a little writing, myself. I'm a newspaper reporter."

Shannon smiled. "A newspaper reporter. Well, Jenice, I'm sure you understand deadlines and editors."

"Sorta'," Jenice shrugged. "I wish I could say I've read your books, but unless you use a pen name I haven't run across them."

"I do use a pen name," Shannon answered, her smile suddenly vanishing. "I'd love to tell you what the name is, but there are reasons I can't."

From the sudden change in Shannon's expression, Jenice knew she had struck a nerve. The reporter in her wanted desperately to pursue the idea. If Shannon didn't want her pen name known, it could only be because she didn't want to be identified. Putting two and two together, Jenice toyed with the idea that Shannon might be living on this island because it was a convenient place to hide. Hide from what?

It took some doing, but Jenice finally forced these thoughts from her mind, deciding to just accept the friendly hospitality these people offered. She could be a reporter again once life was back to normal.

"I hope you'll understand why I need to stay here and write," Shannon said apologetically. "I'd love to go with you to the main island, but . . ."

"Say no more, Shannon. As one writer to another, I understand perfectly."

Brad's boat was a beauty, and a lot bigger than Jenice had expected. It was sleek and red and had a covered cab, providing the driver and his passengers an element of protection from the weather. As Brad started the engine, Jenice toyed with the idea of asking if she could drive. But she put the idea on hold for the time being at least, and just enjoyed the feel of the powerful boat as Brad turned it out to sea and sped away in a burst of acceleration. This little island that could have held so much promise now lay behind her and would soon be out of sight all together. In front of her lay rescue, the return to a life as she had come to accept it in the newspaper world, and the final chapter of Michael Allen—the only man she had ever truly loved.

* * *

"I must admit," Samantha said, after listening to the conclusion of Captain Blake's painful disclosure of his three-hundred-year-old secret, "you do have a stronger case than I had supposed. Not that I think it excuses your little game, because I don't. But—I gave you my word to help clear up your problem, and I always keep my word. You're not the only one who can do that, you know."

Blake wiped away the heavy layer of ghostly perspiration from his ghostly brow, evidence of his inner struggle in revealing his secret for the first time. "Ye be meanin' ye intends to bring this old captain face to face with a blood descendant of Oscar Welborn?"

"I be meanin'—blast it, man!" Samantha scowled. "Now you've got me talking that way. Yes, I'm going to dig out the name of a living descendant, and I'll figure a way of putting you in touch with him— or her—whatever the case. But you have to promise not to give me any more trouble about coming across the line where you belong. Do we have a deal?"

"Aye, lassie, we have a deal. But I beg ye not to be sayin' one word about what yer ears have heard from me tongue this day. Will ye be doin' this?"

"That's part of the deal, Blake. Put your mind at ease. Your secret is locked tighter than the lady's coffin."

Samantha felt a tap on her shoulder and she turned quickly around, surprised to see her husband, Jason, standing behind her.

"Uh—Sam. I hate to bother you when you're working so hard with the captain here, but I'm the bearer of some bad news, I'm afraid."

"What's the matter now? My brother hasn't proposed to that woman again, has he?"

"Sam! This has nothing to do with Jenice. We have an unexpected problem in the making. One the captain here is going to have to handle, since neither you nor I are allowed to go near your brother at the moment."

"And who be this person?" Blake asked pointedly of Samantha. "Ye promised me there would be no interference in our bargain, and now up pops another intruder to me island. I don't like the looks of this, lassie. I don't like it a'tall."

"It's okay, Captain Blake. This is Jason, my cute little ghostly husband. Go ahead, Jason. Tell us what the problem is?"

"The problem is Brad's sister, Shannon. She's in big trouble at the moment, and without Blake's help, it's going to get worse."

Blake's eyes squinted nearly closed. "What sort of trouble be me friend's sister in, matey? And how be I able to help? She be not privy to me existence."

"I'm not sure how you'll handle it, Blake," Samantha said crisply. "But I suggest you found a way quickly. The higher authorities are already a little put out at you. Don't fall on your face now or you may never get up again."

* * *

Having seen the others out the door on their way to Brad's boat, Shannon moved to the kitchen table with her laptop. As she waited for it to power up, a thought came to mind. It concerned the detective in her story. She had given him the name, Shanagon. The more she thought about it, the less she liked the sound of Shanagon. It had to be replaced with a more suitable name. For days now she had been searching her mind for the right name.

For some reason, Michael, the man she had met only this morning, reminded her of the detective in her story. He was handsome—in a rugged sort of way. He was mannerly, and yet he seemed like a man unafraid to face new situations, like coming to this island in a lifeboat. Yes, she would do it. With one command, her computer would search out every mention of the name, Shanagon, replacing it with Michael. She would even keep his last name. Michael Allen was much more suited for the part than Shanagon Basinger.

With that thought in mind, she hit the keyboard. After working ten minutes or so, an uneasy feeling came over her—like she was being watched. But that was impossible. A quick search of the room found her quite alone. She stood and walked to the window, scanning the outside yard. No one there either. Still, the feeling refused to leave. Opening the refrigerator, she removed a pitcher of milk and poured herself a glass. One last look around, and she set the glass of milk next to her work. "Michael Allen," she said aloud. "Yes. Michael will do nicely as my detective."

No matter how hard she tried to bury herself in her story, the strange sensation refused to leave. It grew stronger, until it became almost overpowering. Why hadn't she gone to the main island with the others? It was evident she couldn't write, not like this. With a disgusted sigh, she shut down the laptop and closed the cover. Another look around the yard turned up nothing more than before.

Suddenly, the walls of the house were closing in on her like springs in a trap. Perhaps a walk on the beach would help.

Then, with no warning whatsoever, the back door flew open. There, standing on the threshold, was the dark figure of a man. It took less than one horrifying second for Shannon to recognize him. With an earsplitting scream, she turned to run. But it was too late. In one quick bound he had her wrist in a viselike grip.

"Don't scream, baby," James Baxter said in a calm, cold voice. "You know it makes me upset when you scream."

"Please, James. You're hurting me."

"You don't want me hurting you? You should have thought of that a long time ago. You humiliated me, baby. No one humiliates James Baxter without hurting for it. You'll do your share of hurting, I promise. But not here. You humiliated me in front of the whole world, baby. You're going to make it up to me in front of the world."

"It's been ten years, James. For crying out loud, don't you ever give up?"

"Give up? James Baxter give up? Never, Shannon. I thought you knew me better than that." He gave an evil grin. "I'll bet you're wondering how old James found you, right? Well, baby, old James is no fool. You should have picked a pen name other than Alexis Jenee. That's the name you would have given our daughter, if I'd have let you. Pretty stupid, Shannon. But then you never were known for your great intelligence, were you?"

Baxter pulled her face to within inches of his own. "Speaking of the kid," he spit out. "Where is she? And where is that worthless brother of yours?"

"Tanielle doesn't live here anymore!" she quickly lied. "It's too hard for a fifteen-year-old to live here on this island. She stays with friends, on the main island, where she can go to school and be around others her own age. Michael is here, though. He's just outside, and he has a shotgun."

"You're lying about Michael, and probably about the brat, too. I couldn't care less about her. Michael, on the other hand, could pose a problem. I don't think he's in the house; I've checked through all the windows. And I'd have seen him if he was outside. Tell me the truth, baby. Where is he?"

"All right, all right," she said, her wrist throbbing with pain. "He went out fishing this morning. But he's due back any minute. You know he's not going to let you get away with this."

Baxter let out a sinister laugh. "Do you really think he can stop me? I honestly hope he tries. I'd love nothing better than dealing with Mr. Brad Douglas personally. Not that it matters much. Now that I know where he is, his life isn't worth a cry in the wind. I'll have my boys on him so fast he'll be dead an hour before he even knows it. There won't even be a problem hiding the body in this place. Who's ever going to find it? The growth is so thick out there you could be an inch away and never spot it."

"You're wrong, Baxter. The father of the family where Tanielle stays is with the FBI. I'll be missed and so will Brad. You can't get away with this! Let me go, and get off this island while you still can."

"Oh, I can get away with it, all right, baby." Baxter showed her the leather bag he was holding in his free hand. "Just in case there is any outside interference, I've come prepared with a little insurance."

Dropping the bag to the table, Baxter reached in and removed a roll of gray duct tape. Forcing both of Shannon's hands behind her back, he proceeded to tape them together. As she looked on in horror, he took something else out of the bag. It was a small package wrapped in plain brown paper. This he taped around her midsection. "What are you doing?" she asked, staring nervously at the package. "What is this thing?"

"That little package," he answered cruelly, "contains enough explosives to level this whole house. And this," he said removing one last item from the sack, "is the detonator. You see this little red button? One push, and you're nothing more than vapor in the breeze. Now if you don't mind, I'd like to take my leave of this place. You and I have a boat waiting, baby. I'm taking you home."

* * *

Usually Jenice loved the feel of freedom that came from being on the ocean in a small boat. Sort of like flying in a small plane, compared to an airliner. No one had spoken since leaving the island, and the sound of the humming engine combined with the swishing spray of ocean water rushing past the boat was almost hypnotic. Serene as this all was, it only added to the melancholy already tugging at her heart. She couldn't keep her eyes off Michael, knowing the time would shortly come when she might never see him again. Over and over again, she asked herself the same question: Is the life I've chosen for myself worth giving up someone as special as this man? The answer was always the same: I don't want to end up like my mother.

Suddenly, all her thoughts of Michael were interrupted by the unexpected appearance of Captain Horatio Symington Blake. It was immediately obvious that something was terribly wrong.

"James Baxter be on the island, matey," Blake shouted at Brad. "Shannon be in grave danger, says I. The man be every inch the blackguard ye claims him to be."

"JAMES BAXTER?" Brad shot back. "Of all the blasted luck! How did HE ever find us?"

Brad instantly guided the boat through a long, sweeping turn until they were headed at full speed back toward the island.

Once Jenice had time to catch her breath, something strange began working at her mind. It was the name Blake had used: James Baxter. She was sure she had heard that name before. But where?

CHAPTER 11

As the sleek red boat sped on a beeline course back to the island, the name James Baxter kept ringing over and over in Jenice's mind. Where had she heard the name before? She had already surmised that Shannon lived on this island because she was hiding from someone. From what Blake had told them, it was pretty obvious that someone was James Baxter.

At first, the coincidence of James Baxter showing up on the very day that she and Michael were drawn to this island was a little frightening. After further consideration she concluded it fit the pattern of the other strange events perfectly. Whatever unseen power had been in control of Michael's and her destiny must be at the bottom of James Baxter showing up now.

Jenice glanced at Brad, who was busy driving the boat. Her reporter instincts got the best of her, and she pursued these thoughts by asking him a question. "Who is this James Baxter, Brad? And how is he tied in with your sister?"

Brad never took his eyes off the water in front of them. "James Baxter is Shannon's ex-husband. Shannon left him more than ten years ago, but . . ."

"Let me guess," Jenice continued. "James Baxter was an abusive husband. Shannon tried to walk away from him, but he refused to leave her alone. That's when the three of you packed up and came to this island. Am I getting warm?"

"More than warm, Jenice. You're right on the money. Baxter is a dangerous man. I'm sorry you got mixed up in this, but I have no choice but to go to Shannon's aid. If that madman ever managed to get her off the island, there's no telling what he might do."

"James Baxter!" Jenice suddenly exclaimed. "That's it! He's from San Francisco, right?"

Brad took his eyes off the water just long enough for one quick look at Jenice. "That's right," he said. "Baxter lives in San Francisco. He took my sister there after they were married. But how . . ."

"I'm a newspaper reporter, Brad. I did a story on James Baxter, a couple of years back. I was part of a team who interviewed him in his elaborate San Francisco home. It was a story about his wife, who he claimed had been abducted from his home some eight years earlier. He supposedly had never given up hope of finding her alive, and had spent a small fortune looking for her. That's why I was there, along with reporters from all over. He wanted the story published in the hope it might bring some new leads."

Fire blazed in Brad's eyes. "And you reported the story?" he conjectured.

"I'm a reporter, Brad. Reporting stories like Baxter's is my job."

"That's the problem with reporters," Brad responded coldly. "Every story has only one side. The side that sells to the public. This man is a killer, and you may have helped him find my sister."

"I—I'm so sorry. I'll do anything I can to help."

"I don't need your help, Jenice. The last thing I need right now is to get someone else hurt. When we reach the island, the two of you can stay with Tanielle. If you see she's in any danger at all, you can use this boat to get her as far away from here as possible."

"I be thinkin' matey," Captain Blake broke in. "You'll be needin' more help from these two than watchin' out for the lassie, here. Leave the plannin' to Captain Blake, says I. I've dealt with scoundrels worse than James Baxter long before ye be born."

"You have a plan, Blake? Let's hear it."

Tanielle and Michael had been silently observing these proceedings. Tanielle spoke up now. "Are you talking to your ghost, Uncle Brad?"

Surprise filled Brad's face. "Talking to my ghost?" he gasped. "How do you know about him?"

"I'm not blind, and I'm not stupid, Uncle Brad. I hear you talking to him all the time when you don't know I'm around. He's a sea captain, with a long black beard, and the most stubborn creature you've ever met. I know about his cave, too. I've even seen inside it. It's awesome."

"You've been inside that cave?" Brad shouted.

"Ye've been in me cave?" Blake gasped simultaneously.

"Lots of times. It's where I used to play pirate game with all my imaginary friends. I've never had any real friends on the island, you know."

"Tanielle, that cave is dangerous. You stay away from there, you hear me?"

"Chill out, Uncle Brad. It's no big deal."

"Aye, lassie. Listen to yer uncle. It be extremely dangerous. I was one to learn that fact the hard way."

"Your ghost has seen my father, hasn't he, Uncle Brad? Was that what he was warning you about? Is my mother in danger?"

Michael took the wheel from Brad and gave him a gentle nudge toward Tanielle. Brad didn't argue. Taking Tanielle in his arms, he hugged her tightly. "Your mother will be all right, honey," he whispered. "I won't let your father hurt her, I promise."

"It's okay, Uncle Brad. I know you're a lot smarter than my father. And besides, you have a ghost on your side."

"Aye, the lassie be right, matey. James Baxter is headed straight for the boat he left anchored on the north bank. Yer sister be with him, and she be wearin' some kind of explosive device."

"Explosive device? Baxter has a bomb?"

"That he has, matey. The thing most important, says I, is to be riddin' Mr. James of his transportation."

"Sink his boat, you mean?" Brad asked. "I agree, but how can I sink a boat in the little time I'll have before he reaches it?"

"Me cannon," Blake replied smugly. "That's what cannons be for, matey."

"A cannon?" Jenice asked in shock. "You have a cannon?"

It was Brad who explained. "Blake brought it ashore with him in his longboat when he escaped his sinking ship. He had the idea he might need it for protection. After the two of us struck up a friendship, he had me set the cannon up overlooking the ocean, just for old-times' sake. He even had me come up with powder and balls for the thing. Once a year he has me fire it—on the anniversary of his ship going to the bottom. It makes him happy so I go along with it."

"Aye, and now ye'll be glad ye did, matey. We can use me cannon to blow James Baxter's boat to splinters."

"And you're going to point out where Baxter's boat is anchored, so I can blow it up, right?"

"That be me plan, but not to the letter. We need to stall Baxter long enough to get me cannon armed and ready. That be your job, Brad Douglas. The firin' of the cannon be the job of these two."

Jenice and Michael exchanged glances, and both knew exactly what the other was thinking. "We'll do it," Michael said. "But I've never fired a cannon. I assume you'll show me how."

Brad opened a compartment at the front of the cab and removed a box of water-resistant matches. "All you need is one of these," he said. "The powder, balls, and fuses are stored with the cannon. Blake can talk you through loading and aiming it, then you light the fuse. It's as simple as that."

"What about Tanielle?" Jenice asked. "Shouldn't she remain in the boat? I think that would be the safest thing for her, don't you, Brad?"

"No way," the fifteen-year-old shot back. "My mom's the one in trouble here. I'm going to do my part. I'll go back to the house and keep trying Uncle Brad's radio. Maybe it will start working and I can get some help."

Brad was doubtful. "I don't know, honey. It might be better if you do stay in the boat. You can make your getaway if it comes to that."

"The lassie's right, matey. She'll be safe back at the house, and— luck be with us—she'll be raisin' some help with that talking machine ye be so proud of."

"Listen to your ghost, Uncle Brad. I can be more helpful trying to work the radio."

"Listen to my ghost? You can't hear him, Tanielle. How do you know what he said?"

"Hey, I've heard you talking to him so long now, I know him almost as good as you do. He is telling you to let me work the radio, isn't he?"

Brad looked at the smiling ghost and back at Tanielle. "Well, yes . . ."

"Cool. I'll work the radio."

"After we blow up Baxter's boat," Blake went on to say, "it might be good if ye be coaxin' him to me cave. That be the best place for the ambush I have in mind."

"Are you kidding me, Blake? You're inviting us to your secret cave? Now there's a first."

"What can I say, matey? When under attack, all oars to the water. The cave be the best place, so the cave it must be. I'll be trustin' ye to keep me secret safe."

* * *

"On your feet!" Baxter shouted, yanking at Shannon's arm. "I know a stall when I see one. All the stalling in the world won't do you any good, so knock it off!"

"I tripped, Baxter. What do you expect with my hands bound like this?"

Baxter was right, Shannon was playing the stall game. But not for the reason he might expect. She had given up hope of freeing herself from this monster, but the more time she could give Brad, the better off he'd be. Every second she stalled put Brad's boat one second further from the island, and gave him and Tanielle that much better chance of staying safe. It was funny, she thought, how little fear she felt from this man after all her years of hiding from him. When she had married him, Brad had done everything in his power to convince her otherwise. But no, she was in love. Baxter was older than she was, and she had heard he might be slightly involved with some undesirable people—but he was so exciting and romantic. If only she'd known the man he'd kept hidden behind the mask that came off so quickly after they were married.

She knew, when she came to this island he would be relentless in his search to find her. She also knew the inevitable consequences if he ever did find her. Now the time had come to face those consequences, and her greatest concern was for Tanielle and Brad. Especially Tanielle. Shannon's one big hope was to convince Baxter that revenge on her was enough.

"Which way do I go?" Baxter asked rudely as he came to a fork in the path leading through the thick rain forest. He had had the water tower to guide him in finding the house. He had no such landmark to help find his way back to the beach. "My boat is on the northern shore. Which path leads there?" he demanded.

"The one on the left," Shannon answered, knowing Baxter well enough that he would choose the one on the right. Either path would lead to the north beach, but the one on the right would take a little longer.

Baxter didn't disappoint her. "The one on the left, eh?" he grinned. He shoved her toward the opposite path. "We'll take this one. You're not dealing with a fool, my dear Shannon."

With cruel determination, Baxter forced Shannon along the rugged path until at last they broke free onto the sandy beach. There, as much to Shannon's surprise as to Baxter's, stood the figure of a big man with a rusty red beard. With arms folded defiantly, he stood blocking the way to Baxter's boat. "Hello, Baxter," he said gruffly. "I see you've crawled out from under your rock again. Doesn't the sunlight hurt your eyes out here?"

Baxter stopped in his tracks. "Brad Douglas? Is that really you? As I remember, you used to enjoy staying pretty much in fashion. Ten years on this island has brought some changes in you, I see. I've seen stray dogs with more fashion than you, old friend."

"I'm not your friend, Baxter. Never have been, never will be. And I'm not your brother-in-law anymore, either. The divorce was final years ago. You have no right bothering my sister. Let her go, Baxter."

"Let her go? I think we both know better than that. We both know there's nothing you can do about it, either, don't we, Brad? As usual, I'm holding all the aces."

"What are you going to do, Baxter? Shoot me? Go ahead if you think you can hit anything at this distance. I'm a little out of range, and by the time you come after me I'll be so deep in that rain forest you'll never find me. Not until I pounce on you from out of nowhere. What good will your gun do you then, Baxter?"

Baxter let out a bellowing laugh. "Shoot you? That's not my style, fool. Bullets are too easily traced. I don't mind putting you on hold and letting my boys find a way of finishing you later. Right now I'm more interested in this sister of yours. I have definite plans for her. But, if you insist on giving me trouble, I can forgo those plans and kill her on the spot. You see that package strapped to her waist? One finger on the red button of this detonator, and *boom!* No more sister. Now step aside so we can get to my boat."

"It's not going to do you any good to get to your boat, Baxter. You see, it's not exactly seaworthy anymore." Brad held up the keys to his own boat for Baxter to see. "The only way you have of getting off this island is to use my boat, and that means you have to get these keys from me. I think even you are smart enough not to get stuck on this island with the bodies of your victims laying all over it."

"What do you mean my boat's not seaworthy? What have you done to it, fool?!"

"Just take my word for it, Baxter. That boat isn't going to get you anything but wet."

Obviously confused, Baxter froze in place trying to sort it all out.

"Why did you come back, Brad?" Shannon asked. "You should have just kept going. Come to think of it, how did you know I was in trouble? Wait, don't answer that. I think I know. It was your ghost, wasn't it? The old sea captain warned you, didn't he?"

"My ghost?" Brad asked numbly. "You, too, Shannon? Is there anybody who doesn't know about the captain?"

"How could I help but know? I've heard you talking to him for the past ten years."

"You never said anything about knowing."

"I didn't want to embarrass you, Brad. I saw how hard you worked, trying to keep us from knowing."

"Ghost?" Baxter said. "You think you have a ghost on this island?"

"Oh yes," Brad answered, quickly taking advantage of the situation. "How else do you suppose I knew about you being here? He's a mean one, too. And he hates it when intruders show up on his island. I'd be watching my back if I were you, Baxter. No telling what the captain might have a mind to do."

* * *

"It's a cannon all right," Michael said after pulling off the canvas covering that was used to protect the old weapon from the elements. "So what do I do first, Blake?"

"Open a keg of powder and pour it down the barrel, matey."

There were several small cans on the rock slab not far from the cannon. "You mean one of these?" Michael asked.

"Aye, matey. That be the powder."

"Do I use a whole can?"

"Aye, and be quick about it. Brad Douglas can't be stallin' this culprit forever, ye know."

As Jenice looked on in amazement, Michael opened a can of powder and poured it down the barrel of the old cannon."

"Good, matey. Now tamp it down good with the swab."

"I think he means this," Jenice said, picking up a wooden dowel with a large cloth ball on the end of it.

Michael took the swab from her and used it to force the powder to the lower end of the cannon.

"Now the ball, matey. Put the ball in the barrel and ram it in place like ye be doin' with the powder."

While Michael was working with the ball, Jenice picked up a curled length of fuse. "This looks a little long, Captain," she said. "Should we cut it shorter?"

"Aye, lassie. Cut off three inches or so and shove it in this little hole on the cannon."

"Here," Michael said, handing Jenice his pocket knife after ramming the ball in place with the wooden swab. "Use it to cut the fuse."

Jenice cut off a length of fuse and pushed it into the hole Blake had pointed out. She closed Michael's knife and unthinkingly slid it in the pocket of her blue jeans.

"Well done, ye two," Blake said. "Now all we have to be doin' is aimin' the old fellow at that scoundrel's boat."

Baxter had done his best to hide the boat in some rocks, but it was in plain sight from the hill where the cannon was situated. It took a minute or two for Michael to position the cannon exactly where Blake wanted it. Jenice struck a match and looked at Blake.

"Put the flame to the fuse, lassie. And be ready to cover yer ears. This old cannon's belch be a loud one, says I."

* * *

"You're lying to me, fool," Baxter said, after having time to think. "There's nothing wrong with my boat. Now step aside and let me pass."

At that exact instant, an earsplitting blast was heard from a nearby hill overlooking the beach. The sky went dark with a puff of black smoke. The ball whistled downward, striking the boat dead center. Water and splinters of wood flew violently upward, reaching a height of ten or more feet. Seconds later, the boat sank out of sight.

"Oops," Brad said with a grin so big it was easily seen through his beard. "I guess I wasn't lying after all, huh, Baxter?" Then, before Baxter could gather his wits, Brad broke for the cover of the rainforest and was quickly out of sight.

Baxter stared at the spot where his boat had rested only seconds before. Nothing remained but an oil slick and a few bits of scattered wreckage. From there, his eyes shifted to the hill where the shot had been fired. A large cloud of dark smoke drifted slowly upward into blue of the morning sky. "Who fired that shot?" he demanded harshly. "What was it? A bazooka?"

"It was a cannon," Shannon quickly responded, hoping to keep Baxter from assuming the shot was fired by Tanielle. "We told you the ghost hates intruders on his island. He's been known to do a lot worse things than blow up a boat."

"Shut up! There's no such thing as ghosts. Someone else is on this island." Grabbing Shannon by the upper arm, Baxter pulled her roughly around to face him. "Who is it, Shannon? Tell me, or I'll—"

Baxter was cut off in his efforts by the sound of Brad's voice from out of the thicket. "You want the keys to my boat, Baxter? I'm right here on the path behind you. Come and get them."

Baxter fell silent, and gazed at the path he and Shannon had emerged from earlier.

Shannon forced a laugh. "My brother's right, you know," she pressed. "Your only way off this island now is in his boat. Admit it, Baxter. You haven't a clue how to start the boat without those keys. Kill me, and you'll have nowhere to run."

Baxter wiped the perspiration from his forehead. "I told you to shut up! I have to think." He glanced toward the thicket. "I'll make a deal with you, Brad. Give me those keys, and I'll let Shannon go."

"Like I said," Brad's voice came again. "You want these keys, come and get them."

"Why are you messing with me, Brad? Don't be a fool. One touch of this red button, and Shannon is a dead woman."

"You won't take that chance, Baxter. If that bomb goes off, it won't only be Shannon who's in range of the explosion. You want your revenge, but you're not ready to die for it."

"You're not thinking, Brad. I can shove her aside and dive for cover when I set off the bomb. Don't think for one second I'll hesitate to do it."

"It's you who isn't thinking, Baxter. Kill her, and I'll throw these keys where an army couldn't find them. You'd be stuck here on this island with your victim, and we both know what that means, don't we? Let's talk about a deal here, okay?"

"Deal?" Baxter asked nervously. "What deal?"

"There's a clearing near the center of this island. Shannon can lead you there. I'll meet you there, where we can talk this out face to face."

"How do I know you won't jump me somewhere in that jungle before I ever get to a clearing?"

"How can I do that, Baxter? You have the detonator in your hand. You just said I could never stop you in time. Meet me at the clearing, and we'll talk this out. But you have to toss that gun of yours on the beach where I can see it, or the deal's off."

"What do you take me for, fool? I know you have someone else here on the island. Someone had to fire that cannon. Tell your friend up there on that hill to show himself, and then we can talk about a deal."

* * *

"This guy's insane," Jenice said, as she watched the scene from her spot on the overlooking hill. "We've got to think of something fast."

"Aye, lassie, ye be on the mark. The man doesn't know there be the two of ye."

"You're right, Captain Blake," Jenice agreed. "He doesn't. And if I can convince him I'm alone, it will give us an element of surprise."

"That be me exact thoughts. If we can entice the culprit to the clearin', the matey here can stay hid in the bushes."

Excitement sounded in Jenice's voice as she contemplated Blake's plan. "We just need to find a way to maneuver Baxter into a place where Michael can disarm him. It just might work. Especially if we add one more little weapon to our arsenal. Let me have your wallet, Michael."

"My wallet? What in the world do you want with my wallet, Jenice?"

"I need something in my hand. From this distance Baxter won't be able to tell what it is, and, with a little luck, I might convince him it's a cell phone."

"It might work at that," Michael said, digging the wallet out of his hip pocket.

Jenice reached for the wallet. As she took it from Michael it fell open revealing a picture inside. Jenice was surprised to see it was a picture of her, taken one afternoon in Paris. She looked back at Michael, and as their eyes met her heart started to race. "You still carry my picture?" she asked softly.

Michael swallowed away the lump in his throat. "Yeah, I still carry your picture."

Jenice surprised herself as much as Michael with what she did next. Very slowly, she moved closer. Then, taking his face in her hands—she kissed him. For one brief instant she was in Paris again. The rain, the Eiffel Tower, it was all there—just as it would have been if she had kept her appointment that afternoon. In the channels of her mind she cried out the words, *Yes, I will marry you, Michael Allen. Even if it means a weekly trek to the grocery store is the most exciting adventure I'll ever have again.*

As the kiss faded, so did the fantasy. "I—I'm sorry, Michael," she whispered. "I don't know what came over me. I had no right . . ."

"Oh no," he quickly assured her. "It's perfectly all right."

For the next few seconds they remained with their lips nearly touching. Jenice felt herself engulfed by an almost overpowering desire to bury herself in his arms. Closing her eyes tightly, she backed away and smiled. "It's sweet of you to still carry my picture," she said. "The kiss was just my way of saying thank you. For being so sweet, I mean."

"Yeah, that's what I figured," Michael said.

For a few more seconds the two remained looking at each other. Jenice brushed back her hair, then slowly moved to the edge of the hill until she was in Baxter's sight.

"Hey, fella," she called out. "You want to know who blew up your boat? Well, it was me. I did a pretty good job, wouldn't you say?"

"What? Who are you?" Baxter said, spotting her on the hill.

"Who am I? Boy does that hurt, or what? You don't remember me, Baxter? I was part of a group who interviewed you in your living room a couple of years back. You know, about finding the wife you loved so dearly who had been abducted."

"You're a reporter. I do remember you. What are you doing here on this island?"

"The same thing you're doing, Baxter. Looking for the woman you're holding captive. I was following up on my story, and boy has it taken a strange twist." Jenice held out her hand with Michael's wallet barely visible between her fingers. "You see this cell phone?" she said. "I have the means to reach anyone in the outside world I choose."

"A cell phone?" Baxter asked in shock. "You haven't . . ."

"I haven't called anyone if that's what you were about to ask, Baxter. I'm a reporter, and I smell a story here. Maybe we can work out some sort of deal. I get your story—the real one I mean. Not the fabricated version you gave us all last time."

"And just what am I supposed to get out of this deal?" Baxter asked.

"You get one phone call, to anyone you choose."

"I call someone in my organization to come after me, is that it?"

"Like I say, you get one phone call. Who you call is your business. But you might as well know up front, Shannon isn't going anywhere with you. I'll have no part of any deal that makes me an accomplice to kidnapping."

"All right, all right! I need to think this out. Just don't make any phone calls until the two of us can talk, okay?"

"Fair enough. How about if we all meet in the clearing as Brad suggested?"

"I—don't know about going through that rain forest. Let's meet right here on this beach."

"No deal, Baxter," Jenice responded. "We do it Brad's way or we don't do it at all. I can make a call of my own right now, if you prefer."

"NO! No calls! We'll meet in the clearing."

"All right. But I agree with Brad. I want to see you toss your gun away before we go any further."

Baxter removed the .38 revolver from his shoulder holster, and tossed it to the soft sand a few feet away. "We'll do it Brad's way," he conceded. "But get one thing through your heads. Anything goes wrong—anything at all—and Shannon dies. No matter what else may happen, Shannon dies. Understood, Brad Douglas?"

"Understood," Brad answered from the thicket.

"Show me the way to this clearing," Baxter said to Shannon.

The two of them set out through the rain forest.

CHAPTER 12

"You're sure you know where we're going?" Jenice asked, as Captain Blake led her and Michael through the rain forest along a lesser used path than the one to Brad's house had been. Here, the footing was less sure and walking much more difficult.

"Put yer mind at ease, lassie. Old Captain Blake has walked this here island for the past three hundred years. He knows every rock and root on its soil. This be the right way, says I. Ye have me word on it."

Jenice pushed a particularly stubborn branch out of her face and made her way past it. "Yeah, well, it's a little easier for you to walk over these rocks and roots, Captain Blake. Being an angel gives you a bit of an advantage over us mortals. How long has it been since anyone with flesh and bones came this way?"

"Ye makes a good point, lassie. No one but me friend Brad Douglas ever uses this path, and the times be few even for him. This leads to me cave. The way I be thinkin', no man—nor no woman, fer that matter—has any business at me cave. This occasion bein' the exception, of course. I be knowin' no better place to confront the culprit James Baxter than at me cave—though I'd be obliged if ye and yer friend here keep yer business short and to the point."

Jenice peered ahead. "Speaking of Baxter, what's to keep us from running into him here in the thick of all this growth? Is this the only path that leads to your cave?"

"No, lassie. There be two paths. We be approachin' me cave from the east. The others be approachin' from the west. Brad Douglas be keepin' a close watch on his sister and Baxter, though Baxter be in the dark when it comes to knowin' Brad's whereabouts. We'll be reachin' the clearin' before Baxter. Aye, and that be good, says I. The old capt'n will have time for explainin' his plan."

All her life, Jenice had wished for the chance to explore a deserted island. Never in her wildest dreams would she have supposed an adventure like this one would come along to fulfill that wish. Strange, though. Even with Mother Nature's finest offerings on every side, the thing demanding the biggest place in her mind was Michael's kiss. Why was kissing him so different from kissing any other man? And why did she feel so weak in his arms. It angered her to feel like this.

It reminded her of the time, back in high school, when she had been assigned to the decorating committee for the homecoming dance. She had been a junior that year. Bart Solomon was a senior, and captain of the football team. Every girl in the school idolized Bart Solomon, and most would have given an "A" in social studies for one date with the guy. Jenice was standing on a ladder, hanging crepe paper, when the ladder was bumped, causing her to lose her balance and fall. Of all things, she had fallen right into the powerful arms of Bart Solomon, who had been passing through the gym on his way to football practice. There she was, in Bart's arms, in front of everyone in the room. The others didn't matter at that moment. It was just her and Bart Solomon. Never had she known such a thrill. And never had her strength failed her so completely. Never, that is, until the first time she kissed Michael Allen. Of all the crazy things, to feel so schoolgirlish over a man.

The captain's voice brought her back to the present. "This be the place, mateys. We'll stop here where ye can remain out of sight from the culprit until the time be right for action."

Still hidden by the thick undergrowth, Jenice peered out at the little clearing. The ground at this point appeared to be solid lava rock, which accounted for the lack of vegetation. It was a small clearing, no more than twenty feet in diameter. And sure enough, what looked like the entrance to a cave could be seen near one edge.

"I see why you picked this place," Michael said to the captain. "If we have to confront a man with a bomb, where better could we do it? So, what's your plan, Blake?"

"Once the others reach this point," Blake explained, "the lassie here can step into the clearin' on this side. If she can lure the culprit over here, it will be up to you, matey, to find a way to disarm him without lettin' him blow up Brad's sister. Do you think ye can be handlin' such a chore?"

"I'll have to, won't I?" Michael said.

"Maybe I can be of some help, too," Jenice added. "I do hold a black belt in the martial arts, you know."

"Aye, lassie, but we need yer services in another place. 'It be yer job to free Brad's sister from the bomb that be fastened to her middle with some sort of gray stuff."

"Duct tape," Jenice said. "I still have Michael's pocket knife. I can use the knife to cut the bomb free. All we have to do is separate Baxter from that detonator long enough to get the job done."

"Yeah," Michael grinned. "That should be easy enough to do."

"Hold it down, mateys. They be almost here."

Jenice glanced at the far side of the clearing just in time to see Baxter step into it, holding Shannon tightly by one arm.

"All right!" Baxter yelled out, the detonator clutched tightly in his free hand. "We're here. Show yourselves!"

From seemingly nowhere, Brad stepped out of the jungle into the clearing only a few feet from where Baxter and Shannon stood. "I'm here, Baxter" is all he said.

"All right, now the reporter!" Baxter demanded. "Make yourself visible, lady."

Jenice started to move forward when Michael caught her. She turned to face him. "Be careful," he whispered.

Jenice nodded, then stepped through the growth until she was barely inside the clearing. "I'm here, too," she said.

"All right! All right! Nobody move!" Baxter instructed sharply, and he began edging Shannon to the far end of the clearing, near where the cave entrance lay. "You stay right here, Shannon," he snapped.

Next, Baxter moved away from Shannon to a point near the path they had taken to the clearing. This he obviously did to secure himself a quick retreat if it became necessary. "Take a good look at this detonator," he said, holding it so everyone could see. "One false move, and I push this button. And don't think I won't do it. From here, I can duck to safety in seconds."

"I get the picture, Baxter," Brad said calmly. "So where do we go from here?"

"I want that boat key from you. And I want the cell phone from the lady reporter. Then we can talk about the rest."

"The key is in a safe place not far from here," Brad came back. "We'll talk first, and then see about getting the key to you."

Jenice, who was holding one hand behind her back spoke up. "I'll just hold onto this phone, too. When our deal is finished, I'll make the call for you. Any tricks on your part, and I make a different kind of call than you'd like, Baxter."

Baxter's eyes shifted rapidly back and forth between Brad and Jenice. He was sweating heavily at this point. "Let me see the phone," he spat out.

"I don't think so," Jenice said. "This might come as a bit of a shock, Baxter, but I don't trust you completely. I want my story first. Then I show you the phone."

Baxter wet his lips with his tongue. He forced a smile. "Why wouldn't you trust me, lady?" he said, inching a step in her direction. "I told you the truth in our first interview. You see, I was under the assumption my wife here was abducted against her will. I only recently learned otherwise." As he spoke, Baxter continued to move slowly in Jenice's direction. "Now I learn it was her plan all along. All I want to do is take her home so we can get some help working out our problem. I want to salvage what we've lost and start over. Is that such a bad thing?"

With tightened jaw, Jenice stared at the detonator in Baxter's hand. In an apparent gesture of innocence, he held both hands away from his body as he inched toward her. She saw that his thumb was not over the red button, and she knew why. Any accidental detonation, with him here in the bomb's range, was the furthest thing from his mind. Out of the corner of her eye she could see Michael crouched and ready to spring into action. All she needed was for Baxter to come a couple of steps closer. And he was cooperating nicely, obviously planning a strategy of his own. Little did he know, Jenice was not the pushover Shannon had proved to be.

Baxter paused and stood looking at Jenice for what seemed an eternity. Jenice feared he might not take that one last critical step. Her fears proved unjustified when suddenly he lunged forward in an attempt to grab her, which was a mistake on his part. One well-placed right shoe in his stomach put a stop to that idea. Doubling over in pain, Baxter never saw Michael coming. Michael grabbed an arm and twisted it painfully behind Baxter's back.

Jenice wasted no time. Moving in front of Baxter, she pulled the detonator free from his grip. Quickly, she crossed the clearing to where Shannon stood, and there she gently lay the detonator down on a nearby rock and removed the knife from her pocket. In a matter of seconds, she had the bomb cut free from Shannon. Instinctively, she whirled and threw the bomb inside the cave.

Brad ran to his sister and pulled her to his chest. "Thank heavens you're safe," he said.

"And thanks to our friends here, too," Shannon added. "How about getting this tape off my hands? They hurt something awful."

Just when things seemed to be going right, an unexpected event unfolded. Reaching inside his boot, with his free left hand, Baxter pulled out a small derringer. He immediately pointed it at Michael's head. "Hold it right there, hero!" he shouted. "Let go of my arm or I'll give you a taste of my lead."

Michael stared down the barrel of the two-shot weapon pointed directly at his face. Slowly, he released Baxter, who jumped to his feet and moved quickly away.

A quick assessment of the situation left Baxter believing he was still in full control. Shannon was in her brother's arms, but her hands were still securely taped. Failing to notice the missing bomb, Baxter focused on the detonator where Jenice had left it. He immediately bounded to retrieve it.

"You fools!" he shouted, waving the detonator wildly. "You should know better than to cross James Baxter. Now the lot of you will pay the price. Give me that key, Brad! I'm tired of playing games."

Brad had been cautious enough to leave the boat key hidden a short distance from the clearing. Reaching into his pocket he felt for something, anything that could be used to fool Baxter into thinking it was the key. The only thing in his pocket was some change. Singling out a quarter, he drew it out, keeping it closed tightly in his fist. "You want this key, Baxter?" he half shouted. "Here, catch." With this, Brad threw the quarter into the cave where it noisily bounced from rock to rock until coming to rest on the floor a little ways inside.

"I ought to kill you for that!" Baxter spit out. Shoving the detonator in his back pocket, he grabbed Jenice by the arm, pointing the derringer at her head. "Come on, lady reporter. You and I are going to find that key! The rest of you stay where you are."

Pushing Jenice ahead of him, Baxter made his way into the cave, searching the floor for the key as he walked. A few feet inside, he spotted the quarter lying half under a rock. The light at this point in the cave was poor enough that all he could see was a shiny piece of metal, which he assumed to be the key.

Jenice spotted it about the same time and also assumed it was the key. She knew she couldn't let Baxter get that key. If he did, her life and the lives of the others would be in grave danger. Quickly moving her foot behind his leg, she pushed him with all her strength. It was enough to send him tumbling to the ground, cursing and firing off a wild shot as he fell.

Jenice grabbed the metal object, seeing immediately it was only a decoy. Still, there was one shot remaining in Baxter's gun and he was already halfway up. She made a split-second decision and ran further into the darkness of the cave. Hearing Baxter in close pursuit, she darted behind a large rock and crouched down as far as possible. Suddenly, Baxter's foot hit a protruding rock which sent him tumbling forward over the edge of a deep chasm that was hidden from his view because of the darkness. His lingering scream echoed throughout the cave, until it was abruptly silenced at the end of his fall. In place of his scream came the deafening sound of the exploding bomb near the cave's entrance.

Jenice's last thought before losing consciousness was that Baxter must have landed on the detonator.

CHAPTER 13

Pushing through the door from the viewing room, where she and Jason had been watching the events on the island unfold, Samantha stormed down the hall and into Gus' office where she spotted Maggie at her desk.

"Enough is enough, Maggie!" she shouted. "What have you gotten my brother into, anyway? Gangsters, guns, bombs—I demand you let me go to his aid, now!"

"That won't be necessary, Sam," came a familiar voice from behind her. "There's nothin' ta worry about. I got everthin' under control."

"Gus!" Samantha snapped. "It's about time you showed up. You and I have a few things we need to discuss."

"Yer right, Sam. We do have some talkin' ta do. A lot more talkin' than you might suppose."

"You're behind this whole thing, aren't you, Gus?! Tricking me into thinking we had to use Jenice Anderson to save my brother's life, getting the two of them in that lifeboat, and later on that stupid island. Worst of all, you kept me from being there when Michael needed me! Did you see how that woman kissed him? All I could do was watch. And this James Baxter person!! I want you to get me cleared to go down there, and I want you to do it now! Do you hear me Gus? Now!"

Gus raised both hands, gesturing for Samantha to be calm. "Take it easy, Sam. Like I told ya, everthin's under control. It's all part of a plan I put together with the help of the higher authorities. Ya see, Sam, Maggie and me—"

"Plan you put together? I knew it! You get me authorized now! Don't make me say it again, Gus!"

Gus shrugged. "Sorry, Sam. Ya hafta understand, I can't do that."

Samantha was furious. "What do you mean you can't do it?! You're the Special Conditions Coordinator. It's your job to take care of things like getting approvals."

"That's what I'm tryin' ta tell ya, Sam. I'm *not* the Special Conditions Coordinator. Not any more. The higher authorities took me out of the job."

Samantha's mind went numb. "The higher authorities took you . . ."

"They took me out of the job, Sam. Oh, I have to take care of things until my replacement gets up ta speed, but I'm not allowed ta make any waves. I'm not the one ta be authorizin' anything about yer brother now."

In the face of this immediate crisis, Samantha's concerns about Michael were temporarily laid aside. "What did you do to get the higher authorities upset, Gus?" she asked. "It must have been bad, if they went this far."

"No, Sam, ya got it all wrong. They didn't fire me—they promoted me. I'm movin' up ta the next floor where I'll be in charge of special contracts over a whole universe, 'sted of just one world."

Samantha's face lit up with a bright smile. "A promotion?! Wow!! That's great, Gus."

"Yep, and Maggie's goin' with me."

"All right, Maggie!" Samantha said excitedly. "I'm glad he'll have you there to keep him out of trouble. I cringe to think what havoc a typo in his new job might bring. Who knows, without you as his secretary, he might have some poor fellow born millenniums early. Maybe even galaxies away from where destiny had planned."

"Thanks fer the vote of confidence," Gus grumbled.

"You don't understand, Sam," Maggie explained. "I'm not going to be Gus' secretary. I'm going to be his full-blown partner this time. The higher authorities have concluded I've done as much to run this office as he has, and I deserve it."

"Oh Maggie," Samantha said, rushing over to give her a big hug. "That's wonderful news. When did you find all this out? Wait a minute—does this have anything to do with all the crazy things going on lately? You've known about this the whole time, haven't you? That's why you've been holding things back from us, isn't it?"

Maggie smiled and nodded. "Do you have any idea how hard it's been, not telling you? The higher authorities work that way. They like to keep things from leaking out too soon, and news of the change wasn't officially released until half an hour ago. Gus and I have known for about three weeks now. We've been going through a period of orientation for the new job."

"Congratulations, Gus," Jason said offering his hand. "And you, too, Maggie. I think this is great, and I agree you deserve a shot at being a partner. I have to admit, this is a shocker. I just supposed Gus would be Special Conditions Coordinator forever."

"I practically have been, pal," Gus chuckled. "I've been in the job for centuries now. Longer than anyone before me. It's about time I moved out, wouldn't ya say?"

"That's why all the redecoration to the place," Maggie explained. "We're getting it ready for our replacements. And that's why we've been so busy with the assignments you've been a party to. You see, the higher authorities put it to Gus to get all his clients' matters in order before he leaves the job."

Samantha's smile faded. "*All* his clients?" she repeated. "Like my brother and Jenice Anderson?"

Maggie nodded yes. "Jenice, your brother, Captain Blake, and the others on the island, as well."

"The others?" Samantha asked. "You mean Brad, Shannon, and Tanielle? They're part of Gus' responsibility, too?"

"Oh yes. They're all part of Gus' responsibility. And every one of their cases is filed in the delinquent section. The higher authorities want these cases in order before the job is turned over to someone else."

"Someone else," Samantha said thoughtfully. "I don't suppose you can tell us who that someone might be, can you?"

"What's the matter, Sam?" Gus laughed. "Ya afraid ya won't be able to finagle yer way around the next guy like ya did with me?"

"That might have something to do with it," Samantha offhandedly admitted. "I sort of like these assignments, so long as they don't entail involving my brother with someone like Jenice Anderson. Who knows? I may never get the chance at another one with you gone."

"I wouldn't worry about that Sam. Ya see, the first item of business in our new job is findin' a replacement for this one. Maggie and me had ta come up with a suggestion for the higher authorities. I don't think ya'll have any trouble workin' things out with who we picked."

"All right, Gus. No more games. Either tell us who your replacement is, or tell us it's none of our business, okay?"

Gus grinned and rubbed his hands together mischievously. "What would ya think about yer Granddaddy Collens bein' the new SCC?" he asked.

"Grandad?! Yes! That would be great. But it does pose a question, Gus. Grandad is an angel, like Jason and me. You and Maggie are both advanced past the point of being angels. How can Grandad do the job? I mean, admit it. Time and time again your advanced skills are needed in the job."

Gus shrugged. "Hey, Sam, no problem. I was an angel before I got assigned ta this job. So was Maggie. That's the way it works. One trip ta the higher authorities office, and zap—yer moved up to a second-level angel."

"So Grandad will be like you and Maggie are now?" Samantha asked.

"Well—not exactly," Gus said, obviously skating around Samantha's question.

Samantha's nose wrinkled as she stared at Gus and pondered his meaning. "Not exactly?" she asked. "You're talking in circles, Gus. What's your point?"

"The point is, Sam, yer granddaddy is not the one Maggie and me suggested. Ya see, as we talked it over, we both came ta the same conclusion. If we could be partners in our new job, why not use partners ta fill this one? Ya know what they always say, Sam. Two heads are bigger than one."

"Gus! That should be two heads are BETTER than one. But what are you getting at? Will there be two Special Conditions Coordinators now?"

"That was our proposal ta the higher authorities, and they said yes."

"All right, Gus. If you're trying to confuse me, you've succeeded. How about putting it in plain English. Who are we talking about here?"

Gus folded his arms, spread his grin even wider, and just stood looking Samantha in the eye.

"Wait!" she gasped, as the thought hit her. "You don't mean . . . ?"

"Yep. You and old Jase are fixin' ta go to work. The two of you have an appointment with the higher authorities two hours from now. They approved Maggie and me ta tell ya, but it's up ta them ta make it official."

"The higher authorities?" Samantha cringed. "Good grief Gus, I've never met with the higher authorities. What do I say to them? What do I wear?"

"I'd suggest you wear something nice," Maggie broke in, not trusting Gus to answer this one. "That white dress you wore when you visited your cousins Lisa's and Julie's double wedding reception would be perfect."

"The white dress?" Samantha asked nervously. "What about a green dress, Maggie? I just picked up a new green one over at Casual Universe. Would green be all right?"

"Green would be very appropriate," Maggie agreed.

"My hair! We have to be there in two hours. What will I do with my hair?"

"Your hair is perfect," Maggie assured her. "I don't know how you do it, Sam, but your hair always looks like you just walked out of a beauty shop. Believe me, it's perfect. I wish mine looked half as good as yours. And don't worry about what to say. The higher authorities are easy to work with, I promise."

"Now wait just a darned minute," Jason broke in. "Don't I have something to say about this? I like my job as chef over at the Paradise Palace. I know what I'm doing there, but I'm not sure about this Special Conditions Coordinator thing. I've seen some of the stuff you come up against, Gus, and I don't think I can handle it."

"Hey, pal. The higher authorities have decreed ya get the job. They wouldn't do that unless they were sure ya could handle it."

Jason anxiously rubbed the back of his neck. "So what are you saying, Gus? That I don't have the right to turn the job down?"

"I'm surprised at ya, Jason. Do ya still hafta ask a question like that? Ya know perfectly well the higher authorities never force anyone ta do anythin' they don't want ta do. But they won't like it much if ya do say no."

"But—my job at the Paradise Palace . . ."

Gus shrugged. "Sorry, pal, that one will hafta go. Bein' a SCC is all the job ya'll be able ta handle."

"I like cooking, Gus," Jason insisted.

"Hey, who am I ta argue with that? Ya can fix up one of yer meals fer Maggie and me whenever ya like. I'll bring Joan along, and Maggie can bring Alvin. Anythin' ta keep ya happy, pal."

"What's going to happen to us at this appointment with the higher authorities?" Samantha asked, still scared out of her wits at the thought of actually meeting them.

"They're gonna set up a schedule ta get ya trained in yer new job, Sam."

"We have to go to school? When? For how long?"

"I'm sure they'll want ya ta start right away, and it'll probably take a month ta six weeks ta get ya trained."

"But—what about Michael? He needs me now."

"Not to worry, Sam. Michael's going to be fine. I give you my word, he won't be harmed. And ya can put yer mind at ease about him and Jenice gettin' together without yer help. The higher authorities are a little concerned about yer attitude regardin' Jenice. They've made it clear you're the one responsible for that particular contract, and now I can tell ya the rest of the story. Ya'll be handlin' yer part of sealin' their contract as a second-level angel, Sam. That will be yer first assignment in yer new job."

"But, Gus—"

"Sorry, Sam. I can't help ya with this one. The higher authorities took it outa my hands."

"Gus is right, Sam," Maggie said. "You can't argue with the higher authorities. And you have to understand, they do know what they're doing. Every time."

Samantha's head was spinning like the inside of her grandmother's old washing machine. What had been a big enough problem, of finding a way to tactfully get Jenice Anderson out of Michael's life, had now escalated into one next to impossible. And if that wasn't enough to worry about, now there was the thing of meeting the higher authorities—and going to school for the next several weeks—and—oh my gosh—and—being the next Special Conditions Coordinator. It was overwhelming. She had wanted an excuse to show off her new green dress, but this was ridiculous.

CHAPTER 14

Captain Blake looked on in disbelief as smoke and dust billowed out of the mouth of his cave. What had this culprit done? The cave was not only Blake's tomb; it also held the map to his cherished secret. Not to mention what might have happened to Jenice, who was inside the cave with Baxter. As the captain contemplated checking inside to see how serious the blast had been, a very strange thing occurred, one of the strangest he could ever remember seeing. Everything came to a sudden standstill. The smoke and dust hung in midair, the people next to him froze in place, even the noise from the explosion instantly went silent. "By the stars," Blake said to himself. "What be happenin' here?"

Then he noticed a movement at the edge of the clearing. As he watched, a man stepped from the thicket and approached him. "It's okay," the newcomer said. "I'm Gabe, and I've put time on hold 'til I get my job done here."

"Gabe?" Blake asked. "Do ye be from the other side?"

"Yep. I'm here for a pickup. That's my job, Captain Blake."

Blake's left eye squinted nearly closed. "A pickup, ye say? But it's not me ye be after. Ye be aware of me stand on the matter, be ye not?"

"Relax, Captain. I'm not here for you."

"A thousand curses, says I. You be here for the lassie. She be killed by the blast."

"No, I'm not here for the woman, either. She's not my responsibility. I pick up the other kind, like him," Gabe said, pointing toward the cave.

Blake looked back to the cave where he saw what was left of James Baxter making his way out of the rubble, hands over his ears, and looking more than a little stunned.

"Oh, my ears," Baxter groaned. "What happened in there?"

"You set off the bomb," Gabe explained. "When you fell into that cavern."

"What is this?" Baxter demanded, noticing Gabe and Blake for the first time. "Where did you two come from?"

"Name's Gabe," the official greeter smiled. "This here's Captain Horatio Symington Blake. He's sort of the resident ghost on this island."

Baxter looked confused. "My gun!" he cried, realizing he was now unarmed. "I've got to get to that gun." Searching out the path that led back to the beach, he attempted to reach it. To his complete dismay, he found he couldn't move. His feet were glued to the ground. "What is this!" he shrieked. "What's holding my feet?"

"Wouldn't you know it?" Gabe shrugged. "A stubborn one. I was hoping for an easy pickup. Well, I guess a demonstration is in order. What'll you have, Baxter—a lightning bolt, a dozen angels with drawn swords, or perhaps a quick peek at where it is you're bound for?"

Baxter struggled all the harder to free himself, with no more success than before. "What are you rambling on about?" he spat out. "Lightning bolt? Angels with swords? You're insane."

Gabe rubbed his fingers over his chin. "Aaah—let's try something simple and see if that won't do the trick." He pointed a finger at Baxter, who could only watch as a streak of light shot out, striking him exactly on the tip of his nose.

"Yikes!" Baxter screamed in pain, grabbing his nose and staring back at Gabe. "Who are you?! What did you hit me with?!"

"I'm your official greeter," Gabe responded. "I'm here to escort you to your appointed destination. My little zapper is just a way of helping to convince you to come along without giving me a big hassle about it."

"I be glad yer not the one who came after me, matey." Blake observed. " Ye be havin' a bit of a mean streak about you."

"Nah, I'm not all that mean. Not really. It's just that the sort I'm assigned to pick up sometimes need a little persuading. You didn't fall into his category, Captain Blake. Not that you didn't give your greeter a handful of trouble, and not that he couldn't have been more force-able in your case, but still—you weren't in the same category as Baxter here. But then, where he's going holds a lot less to be desired than what awaits you, when you finally give in to your greeter."

For the first time, Baxter took a good look at what was going on around him. "Why are all these people acting like wax dummies?" he asked sharply. "And if the bomb went off, why is Shannon still in one piece? I demand to know what this is all about!"

"I told you, Baxter. You just weren't listening. That's the trouble with guys like you, you just never learn how to listen. Read my lips. I'm your official greeter. The time has come for you and me to take a little trip to your new home. Not that you're going to like it much, but that's the breaks. You're the one who signed on the bottom line assuring yourself a spot in the place."

Baxter tried again to lift his feet. They still refused to budge. "Why are all these people frozen in their tracks while you and Long John Silver here are moving around completely normal?" he asked in confusion.

"Well, Baxter. It's a little bit complicated. I have time on hold, you see. That means that anything subject to time as it applies to this place is at a standstill. Will be till I start time up again. It doesn't affect me because I'm the one in charge. It doesn't affect Captain Blake here, because he's not part of this place. Not technically, anyway. He's what you might call a ghost."

"A ghost?" Baxter echoed. "Preposterous! There are no such things as ghosts."

Gabe scratched the back of his head. "Well now, Baxter, I wouldn't be saying things like that if I were you. You see, you yourself are a ghost now. Here, let me show you what I mean."

Gabe bent down and picked up a small lava rock, which he tossed over to Baxter. Instinctively, Baxter reached out to catch the rock, only to see it slip through his hands as if they weren't there. Wide-eyed, he stared at his own hands. "You mean I'm . . ."

"You're dead, Baxter. Now are you ready for the trip?"

"What trip?! I don't want to go anywhere!"

"Well, be that as it may—you have to go. It's the law, Baxter. And this particular law is one you and your cronies can't bend."

Baxter tried harder to free himself. "Where are you taking me?" he barked.

"It's just a place, Baxter. A place where you can begin paying a debt you've been stacking up over the last few years."

"You mean—you're taking me to prison?"

"I don't like that word, but it does get the general idea across, I suppose. Oh, and I've heard you say on several occasions there was never a prison built that could hold you, Baxter. But," Gabe shrugged nonchalantly, "I think this one will do the job. There's never been a breakout yet, and there's never been a highfalutin' lawyer who managed to shorten the stay for any of our guests. Not even by one day. Now what do you say we be on our way, Baxter? Your destiny awaits."

"No!" Baxter shouted. "I can't be dead! There has to be some mistake!"

"Come on, Baxter," Gabe pleaded. "Don't make me use that lightning bolt."

Blake spoke up. "I think ye had better be listenin' to this bloke, James Baxter. He be tellin' the truth about the lightnin' bolt. And if ye be thinkin' the little shot to yer nose be hurtin', a lightin' bolt is a mite bigger, says I."

Gabe reached a hand out to Baxter, taking him by the shoulder. At the touch of Gabe's hand, Baxter's feet pulled free from the power holding them.

"Come on, let's get going." Gabe said with authority in his voice. "If there's one thing I hate in these cases, it's long good-byes."

Blake watched as the two of them moved toward the edge of the rain forest. "What about the bright light, matey?" he asked of Gabe. "I be seein' this done before, and there always be a bright light."

"There's no bright light for this type, Captain Blake. They get no fanfare at all." Gabe let out a long, lingering sigh. "Sometimes I wish I could be a greeter for the good ones. This gets a little depressing at times. But someone has to do it."

With this, Gabe stepped into the thicket pushing Baxter in front of him. No sooner had the two disappeared from sight, than time resumed its normal flow. The noise of the blast picked up where it had been cut short. The smoke and dust again swirled mightily through the atmosphere in the clearing. And the people were once again moving.

"Aye," Blake said to himself. "That be an experience, says I. When me time does roll to the surface, I hope it be not Gabe who picks me up."

CHAPTER 15

Michael stood stunned. The blast had been deafening, with an earth-shaking jolt to match. And he was outside the cave. What must it have been like inside? Little by little, the reality of what had happened came together in his mind. His heart pounded. His mouth went dry.

"JENICE!" he cried at the top of his voice. Rushing to where the cave entrance had been only seconds earlier, he cried out again. "CAN YOU HEAR ME?!! ARE YOU ALL RIGHT?!!!" All hope began to waver when there was no answer. "PLEASE, JENICE!" he cried again. "SAY SOMETHING! ANYTHING!" His voice tapered off. "Just let me know you're alive. Please let me know you're alive."

"She be alive, matey. Of that much I be sure."

Michael's attention shifted to Captain Blake. "You can see her?!" he pressed.

"Aye. I can see her. She be unconscious and bleeding about the head. But she be breathin', matey."

"I've got to get to her! There's so much rubble . . . can you tell how far it extends, Blake? Can we get through it?"

"It be not deep, matey. A cannon's length. Maybe two, but no more, says I. Ye can break through, I feels it in me bones."

Michael wasted no time. Dropping to his knees, he pulled out one rock, and then another, and another. As each rock was dislodged, he threw it a few feet to one side.

"Move over," Brad barked, diving in next to Michael. "Four hands are faster than two."

"How about me?" Shannon asked. "What can I do to help?"

"We need a flashlight, sis," Brad answered. "And my first-aid kit. You can run back to the house and bring them."

"How about some water and towels?" Shannon suggested.

Brad nodded. "Good idea. And a blanket or two wouldn't hurt. Hurry. With luck, we could be through this heap a lot faster than you might think. Oh, and you might bring my shotgun, just in case Baxter is still in the mood for trouble."

Captain Blake let out a gruff laugh. "There'll be no need for the shotgun, matey. James Baxter won't be givin' you any more trouble. Ye has me word on it."

Brad looked confused. "What are you saying, Blake? Baxter is still in the cave, isn't he?"

"No, matey," Blake explained. "Baxter's bones be in the cave, but the rest of him be gone."

"What do you mean, Blake? Is Baxter dead?"

"Aye, he be dead, all right. With me very eyes I saw him dragged off to his place of waitin'. Cryin' all the way, he was. Aye, but his bones be there at the bottom of the cave, layin' straddled across me own. I'll not rest till I be findin' a way to move the culprit's last remains. I'll not be sharin' me grave with the likes of him, by thunder."

"Baxter's dead," Brad repeated, without the slightest hint of remorse. "Did you hear that, sis? Baxter's dead. You know what that means? It means you're free to live out the rest of your life the way you deserve. You can go home, Shannon. There's nothing in this world holding you back now."

Shannon stared expressionless at her brother. "Baxter's dead, you say? How do you know, Brad? Did your ghost tell you?"

"He did. Are you hinting you don't believe him?"

Shannon didn't answer right away. When she did, she said, "I'll believe Baxter's dead when I see his cold, lifeless body with my own eyes. Time and again I thought the man was out of my life, but somehow he's always managed to come crawling back. If you'll excuse me, I'd better fetch the things from the house. My apologies to your ghost, Brad—but I'm bringing the shotgun back with me."

Brad watched as his sister disappeared into the rain forest, then with a sigh, he returned to his digging.

"If it's any of my business, Michael," he asked, "are you and Jenice just good friends, or does it go deeper than that?"

"I asked her to marry me once," Michael explained, never slowing at his task.

"She turned you down then?"

"I guess you could say she turned me down. She asked for some time to think about it. Then, she simply walked out of my life. No word of explanation, no nothing. I just looked around and she was gone."

Michael glanced over at Brad. "How about you? Was there ever anyone special in your life?"

"Oh yes," Brad replied with an obviously forced smile. "There was Lori. Only with Lori, I just looked around to see she had found someone else."

"I'm sorry," Michael said. "I think I have some idea of how much it hurt." After a moment's thought, he added, "Though I've often wondered if it wouldn't have been easier losing Jenice like that, instead of the way it happened."

"It's six of one and half a dozen of the other," Brad sighed. "Either way—life goes on."

Michael feigned a laugh. "Yeah, darned if it doesn't. You on your isolated island, and me chasing rainbows all over the world."

Brad posed another question. "So how did the two of you happen to be together in that lifeboat? Sorry to pry, but my curiosity is killing me."

"How did we happen to be together in the lifeboat? That, Brad, is a long, and a very unbelievable story." Michael glanced up at Blake. "Come to think of it, you're a little used to the unbelievable, Brad. I'll relate the story, if you like."

"I'd love to hear it, Michael. If you're sure you don't mind."

* * *

Shannon pushed open the door and stepped inside the house. "Tanielle," she called out. "Where are you?"

"In here, Mom. In the radio room. Get in here. There's something you should hear."

Shannon went directly to the room, where she spotted Tanielle at the radio. "What is it, honey?" she asked. "Have you managed to reach someone?"

"No. I can hear people talking, but I can't answer them. We have another problem, Mom. There's a storm coming. An awesome storm, according to the reports."

"Storm?" Shannon asked, a bit surprised. "I haven't heard about any storm, and it certainly doesn't look like a storm's brewing."

"All I know is what I've been hearing. The officials on Saint Thomas Island have been trying to reach Uncle Brad, but they can't hear me answering."

Shannon moved closer to the radio so she could hear the reports for herself. Tanielle was right. A storm was reportedly blowing in from the Atlantic with winds exceeding 160 miles per hour. All boats were being called ashore, and the people were being advised to seek places of strong shelter.

As she listened, one of the operators tried again to reach her brother. "Brad Douglas," came the voice from the speaker. "If you can hear me, take warning, my friend. That little island you're on is dead in the path of this thing. Get out of there, friend, and do it fast! Head for Saint Thomas, where you and the girls can hole up in a school house or church building. I'm not kidding you, buddy. This storm is fixing to be one big blow."

A cold chill ran through Shannon's veins at these reports. Under better circumstances, she could simply tell Brad about the storm and they would be on their way to Saint Thomas. But with Jenice trapped in the cave and possibly hurt, it wasn't that simple. They couldn't just leave her there. She toyed with the idea of having Tanielle go to Brad's boat while she returned to warn the others. If bad came to worst, Tanielle could at least save herself. But what if she failed to beat the storm? Thoughts of Tanielle alone in a boat, with a hurricane on its way, were too frightening to chance such a thing. She'd just have to play this out one step at a time, and hope for the best.

"Grab your rain gear, honey," she told Tanielle. "I've got some things to gather up, then we can go back to the cave where Uncle Brad and the others are waiting."

"What about my dad?" Tanielle asked worriedly.

"Your dad can't hurt us anymore, honey." Even though Shannon wasn't absolutely positive herself, she felt it best to say this for Tanielle's sake.

"Awesome!" Tanielle cried out. "I knew Uncle Brad could handle him. Did he beat him up, or what?"

"I'll explain later. Just get your rain gear, and wait for me at the front door, okay?"

* * *

Drawing in a deep breath, Jenice looked up at the lovely evening Paris sky. It was a great evening for a walk. Especially here, on the Pont des Arts, a pedestrian bridge overlooking the beautiful Seine River. Even more especially, since this walk was in the company of someone as special as Michael Allen. There was no denying it; Jenice was falling in love and it felt wonderful.

"You know what I want to do?" Jenice laughed, releasing Michael's hand and stepping to the railing's edge where she could get a good look at the river flowing beneath them. "I want to bungee jump off this bridge. How 'bout it, Michael? Are you game to do it with me?"

Michael laughed. "I don't think so," he said, coming up behind her and wrapping his arms around her waist. "We need a higher bridge for bungee jumping."

"Why do we need a higher bridge? We can just use a shorter cord. I'll bet no one has ever bungee jumped off this bridge. We could be the first, Michael. You know how important it is for me to be first at whatever I do."

"A short bungee cord? You're crazy, you know that, Jenice? Why not just dive off the bridge, clothes and all, and go for a moonlight swim. I mean, we're going to get arrested anyway. Why fool with rounding up a bungee cord?"

"I don't know," Jenice objected. "That water looks pretty cold. If I'm going to be arrested, I'd just as soon be comfortable. I vote we bungee jump and stay dry."

"I've got a better idea," Michael said, gently turning her around to face him. "I say we set a record for the longest kiss ever on this bridge." Before Jenice knew what was happening, Michael pulled her into a kiss.

Ummm, she thought to herself. *He's right. This is a bigger kick than bungee jumping off the bridge.*

Wonderful as the kiss was, something about it just didn't seem right. Somehow it all seemed so distanced. So unreal. Sort of like a dream. Then a light struck her in the face. She broke the kiss to see where the light had come from. It seemed to be coming from some sort of spotlight on an approaching boat. It was so bright, it hurt her eyes. And what was that sound? It was—her name. Someone was calling her name, but who? And why did the voice seem to be coming from so far away?

Jenice stared at the spotlight only to realize it was no spotlight at all. It was—of all things—a flashlight. Someone was holding a flashlight in her eyes, and they kept calling her name.

"Jenice, speak to me. Are you all right?"

It was Michael's voice. But where did he get the flashlight? And where was the bridge? Where was the river? This was all wrong.

"Where—where am I?" she managed to ask with great difficulty.

"You're in a cave," Michael explained. "There was an explosion."

Jenice struggled to focus her eyes. Slowly, Michael's face came into view. "I'm in a cave?" she gasped. "There was an explosion?"

"That's right, a big explosion. You were only feet from the center of the blast. How do you feel? Can you move your fingers? Your feet?"

"I—I think so," Jenice said, testing her limbs one at a time. "But I have a headache you can't believe. And my mind is so—fuzzy."

"You have a nasty cut on your forehead, but thank goodness it's at least stopped bleeding."

Jenice made an effort to sit up. She made it, but only with Michael's help. "Why am I in a cave? What happened to the bridge?"

"Bridge? What bridge, Jenice?"

"You know. The bridge. The Seine River. We were going to bungee jump—and then the boat was there with that bright light." She paused, trying to bring the pieces together in her mind. It was so hard, like trying to see through a dense fog on a winter's day in balmy old London. "You kissed me, Michael. Why did you stop? We were going to set a record. Oh yes—the boat with the light. That's why you stopped, isn't it?"

Michael placed the flashlight on a rock where it gave enough light to see fairly well. He pulled out the towel he had shoved inside his shirt before crawling into the cave. Very gently, he cradled her head in one arm while wiping away some of the dried blood and grime from her forehead.

"The things you describe," he softly told her, "didn't just happen, Jenice. The day we talked of bungee jumping from the Pont des Arts was a very long time ago, and in a different world."

Jenice struggled to make some sense out of Michael's words. What did he mean it had been a long time ago? It was only a minute or so ago. She could still feel the warmth of his lips on hers. Why was she in this cave? Her eyes settled on Michael's face, and suddenly nothing else mattered.

He was strikingly handsome, even here with so little light. She loved the color of his hair, so blond it was nearly white. And she loved those big bushy eyebrows. She loved everything about his face—everything about him—no, it went even further than that—she loved HIM. The temptation was just too great. Reaching a hand behind his head, she pulled him into a kiss. The bridge was gone, as was the river. But who cared? The kiss was there, just as warm and exciting as ever.

After a moment, she felt him pull away. "Listen to me, Jenice," he quietly whispered. "You've had a bad blow to the head. I'm afraid you may have a concussion. Tell me, what's the president's name?"

"The president?" Jenice frowned. "I don't know what his name is. Who cares? I probably didn't vote for him, anyway." Jenice lay a hand to her own head. "Oh, it hurts," she complained. "You said there was an explosion?"

"You were trapped in this cave. It took two of us more than half an hour to dig through the rubble caused by the blast."

"Baxter?" she said, forcing her mind back to the present. "He hit the detonator?"

"Yes, that's right, Jenice. You were inside the cave with Baxter when the bomb went off."

Things still refused to focus in Jenice's mind, but the name Baxter was there, along with his bomb. "This cave," she said. "The walls may have been weakened by the explosion. The whole place could come crashing down on us."

Michael looked around them. "It's possible, I suppose. But it looks fairly stable. Everywhere except where we dug a tunnel into the place, that is. I'm not sure how stable that part may be."

Jenice leaned forward and kissed Michael one more time. "You came after me," she whispered. "You could have been killed, but you came."

"Had to," he smiled. "You still have my pocket knife, remember?"

His knife? She lay a hand to her pocket and felt the knife still there. "I do have your knife, don't I?" she laughed. "That's why you came after me."

Laughing made her head hurt so bad—but she didn't care. She kissed him again and stroked his hair with her fingers. Like so many times before, she wanted to tell him how she loved him. But just like all the other times—the words refused to cross her lips.

Michael stood and helped Jenice to her feet.

"What's the matter?" she complained. "Don't you like kissing me anymore?"

"Of course I like kissing you, Jenice. I'd like it more if it were the real you I was kissing, and not the you so dazed you can't even remember the president's name. But we really do have to get out of here. We have to get you some medical help, and they say there's a big storm on the way. There's no time to waste."

Jenice managed to walk with a lot of help from Michael. It took only a short time to reach the point of the cave-in. Jenice stared at the tiny hole dug through the debris. It looked so tight and had to be at least four feet through to the outside. "I don't know if I can make it through that little hole, Michael," she said, holding her aching head in one hand. "I don't feel very good right now."

"You have to make it through, Jenice. It's the only way out, and time's burning on us."

Michael leaned his face into the opening. He could see Brad looking back from the other end. "She has a concussion, Brad," Michael said. "She'll need some help getting out."

"Send her on," Brad quickly responded. "I'll help her all I can on this end."

Michael stood again. "Okay, here we go," he said, helping her into the opening. "If I can make it through, so can you."

With her head pounding like a Comanche war drum, she started through the hole. With Michael pushing her from behind, she quickly spotted Brad's outstretched hand in front of her. She strained to reach his hand, and at last felt his iron grip on her wrist. In a matter of seconds, she was outside. The fresh air felt wonderful to her lungs, and even helped clear her head somewhat. She still couldn't remember the president's name, but at least she did remember each of these faces. There was Brad, Shannon, Tanielle, and that old sea captain. What was his name? And what was it about him that was so different from the others? There was something. She knew there was something, but just couldn't get straight what it was. She turned just in time to see Michael emerge from the makeshift cave entrance.

"Please tell me Baxter's not coming out of that cave," Shannon said, the anguish obvious in her voice.

"There's no worry about that," Michael assured her. "I saw the gorge he fell into while I was looking for Jenice. Take my word for it, Shannon. You're free from that man. He'll never bother you again."

"Thank goodness," she sighed. "I hate to think dying was the only thing that would force him to leave Tanielle and me alone, but . . ."

Brad slid an arm around Shannon. "It's all right, sis. Captain Blake tells me he was there when Baxter was escorted away to his new habitat. Who knows, maybe he can find himself a new life over there. I do know you and Tanielle can find yours now. So far as I'm concerned, that's the important thing."

Shannon pulled Tanielle into the circle, and the three of them hugged. "Make that all three of us who can find our lives again," she wept. "You're just as important as we are, Brad. Maybe even more important. None of this was your fault from the beginning."

Brad shrugged it off. "Ah, let it go, sis. What difference does a few years on this island make to a man who has so little left in the outside world, anyway?"

"Meaning Lori?" Shannon asked.

"Meaning Lori," Brad sighed.

"You'll find another, Brad. Someone who will make you very happy. I just know it."

Brad stepped away and turned his attention back to Jenice. "We've got to get you off this island fast, young lady," he said.

"There's a big storm blowing in. If we hurry, we should be able to reach Saint Thomas before the worst of it hits. It's going to be a bit of a rough ride, I fear. But what other choice is there? None of us would be safe on this island, and besides we have to get you to a hospital."

Even before Brad finished his sentence, a new sound was heard in the distance off to the north.

"Is that what I think it is?" Michael shouted.

"If you're thinking helicopter, then it's what you think it is, Michael," Brad came back. "They must be looking for the girls and me. When we didn't answer the radio, they must have become concerned."

"A helicopter," Michael repeated. "That means a faster way of getting help for Jenice."

"Not to throw cold water on your hopes," Brad said. "But they'll be looking for us over by the house. They'd have to be directly overhead in order to spot us here in this small clearing. I'd better head that way. It'll be close but maybe I can reach them before they give up and leave."

"No, wait!" Michael shouted, grabbing up the double-barrel shotgun Shannon had insisted on bringing back from the house. "I think we can signal them."

Brad shook his head. "It won't work, Michael. The noise in that helicopter will easily drown out the noise of a shotgun blast."

"I'm not interested in the shotgun," Michael explained, breaking open the breach and removing a shotgun shell from each barrel. "I'm interested in these." He held up the shotgun shells for all to see. "I still have the matches you gave me to set off the cannon. With the powder from these shells, we can start a fast signal fire."

"Good thinking," Brad shouted, as the noise from the approaching helicopter grew closer. "We'll burn one of these blankets. It'll make the most possible smoke."

"The knife," Michael said to Jenice. "Let me have it."

Jenice dug the knife out of her pocket and handed it to Michael. "You really must love this knife," she chuckled. "You'll go to any length to get it back."

"I do love the knife, Jenice. You gave it to me, remember?"

Jenice watched as Michael dug open the end of one shotgun shell to get at the powder.

I did give you that knife, didn't I? she reasoned with great effort. *It was earlier on the same day you asked me to marry you. The day I promised to meet you in one week at the Eiffel Tower. I remember now. It's all coming back. You've kept that knife all this time? Maybe you do still love me, Michael. Maybe you do.*

Brad crumpled a blanket and lay it on the ground in the center of the clearing. Michael then dumped the gunpowder on one edge and set a match to it. The powder instantly burst into flame, igniting the blanket in the process. In less than a minute, the combined efforts of Michael and Brad had paid off. They had a fire going. A fire, and lots of dark smoke, which was precisely what they wanted.

CHAPTER 16

The two men had to shout to be heard over the sound of the helicopter.

"I'm telling you, Jenkins, this is a stupid idea. We don't have time for this. We need to get this chopper on the ground before the storm hits, and it's not that far away."

"Just one pass over these people's house, Bob," Roy Jenkins insisted. "I need a shot of what the place looks like now, so we can come back later and get a comparison shot of what it looks like after the storm. Who knows, we might even spot your friends, and you can be a hero. I guarantee you a spot on the five o'clock news if that happens."

Roy Jenkins was well known for being an aggressive news reporter who often brought along his own video equipment. This storm was big news. What great luck that he had been on the scene when this big blow came out of nowhere. He'd scoop everyone on this story, for sure. Roy had pumped Bob Rivers, the chopper pilot, for everything he could get. When he learned there were three people living on this tiny island, nothing would do but get here to shoot some footage. Before and after shots were always one of Roy's favorite formats.

"I don't want to be on the five o'clock news," Bob protested. "I just want to set this bird on the ground and get home where I can be with my family through this thing."

Roy refused to back down. "What's it going to take, two minutes? Look, there's the house now." The reporter brought the camera into position and began shooting. "Keep her as steady as possible, will ya, pal? This has all the makings of a great shot."

Bob had no heart for what he was doing, but as long as he was here he thought it wouldn't hurt to take a look around for Brad and the girls. Bob and Brad were good friends, and he knew the people on the shortwave had not been able to raise anyone from the island.

"They must still be here," he offhandedly remarked. "There's Brad's boat docked down there."

"Hey!" Roy cut in. "You want to hold it down, please. This camera does have sound, you know. I'll do the talking, you just fly."

Roy started the camera again, along with a line of reporter jargon describing the visual scene the camera was recording. Bob paid little attention as he scoured the area for signs of life. After one pass over the house, he flew back and hovered at one point to give Roy a good shot of the whole area. Roy continued shooting while he gave a running verbal commentary. After a few minutes, Roy lowered the camera.

"Okay," he said. "We can go now. I'll see to it you get a little something extra on your check for your cooperation."

Bob adjusted his baseball cap and set the chopper in motion back toward Saint Thomas Island, his home base. Then, just as he reached the shoreline, something caught his eye. "Look, over there!" he called out sharply. "Is that smoke I see?"

"Yeah, it is," Roy agreed. "What do you make of it, Bob?"

"I don't know, Jenkins, but I'm going to get a closer look, that's for sure."

"Now you're talking my language," Roy barked, bringing the camera back into position.

* * *

If Jenice ever had an Excedrin headache, it was now and the bright light of the morning sky did nothing to help. She kept a hand across her eyes and left the tracking of the helicopter to the others. She did manage a look, though, when she heard Michael's shout.

"They've seen us! They're turning around. I knew the smoke would do the trick. I just knew it!"

"We're not out of the woods yet," Brad warned. "That's Bob Rivers' chopper. I'm familiar with it. The most you can cram in it is five people, and that's with Tanielle sitting on someone's lap. Even if Bob is alone in the chopper, that still leaves one of us out. And if that storm is as close as they say, there'll be no time for a second trip."

"Just leave me the keys to your boat, Brad. I'll take my chances that way, and let the rest of you go in the chopper."

"No deal, Michael. I'm the one to take the boat. I know these waters better than you. Don't say another word; my mind is made up."

"I cut my teeth doing tougher things than piloting a boat through a few big waves," Michael persisted. "I'll take the boat. You go in the chopper."

As the chopper drew near it became evident that Bob wasn't alone. He had a camera man with him. "Well it looks like the argument is settled," Brad observed. "We can both go in the boat."

Michael took a closer look, only to confirm what Brad had seen. "Looks like," he said. "But at least the girls have a ride out of here. That way they'll be relatively safe, and Jenice can get some medical assistance faster."

"Stand back!" Brad shouted. "Bob is putting down in the center of the clearing. Give him all the room possible."

Jenice was amazed at the skillful manner with which the chopper drifted downward into the small clearing. The wind from the blades blew dust and debris everywhere, not to mention what it did to her already stringy hair. In her muddled mind, she strained to think what it might mean for her to go on the helicopter and Michael to stay behind and join her later. Or would he join her later? Maybe the two of them would become separated through all this. It was an unpleasant thought, for the moment, at least.

The chopper touched down, and the blades slowed to idling speed. The pilot remained at the controls, but yelled out the window at Brad. "Why are you still here on the island? You should be at least halfway to Saint Thomas by now. And who are these other people with you?"

Even with the chopper blades at idle, the men had to yell to hear each other. "It's a long story, Bob. But we have a situation here. The lady over there has a concussion. How fast can you get her to a hospital?"

"She has a concussion? How bad?"

"Pretty bad, I'd say. She can't remember the president's name."

Bob thought a moment. "Offhand, I'd say I should hightail it for Key West. All the medical people on Saint Thomas are going to be pretty busy."

"Key West?" Brad asked. "Can you beat the storm that far?"

"I'll be in front of the storm, moving in the same direction it's moving. I shouldn't have any problem. I won't have time to let anyone off at Saint Thomas on the way, though. If Shannon and Tanielle come with me, it will be all the way to Key West. I'll have to radio my family about what's happening. Much as I hate to admit it, they're used to it."

"Hey, wait just a darn minute," Roy objected. "I want to get these pictures on the wire fast."

"Forget it, Roy. We've got a woman hurt here. That takes priority."

Roy lowered his camera and took a good look at those standing outside. His eyes came to rest on Jenice. Suddenly, his jaw dropped open. "Jenice Anderson?" he said. "Can it be . . . ?"

Pushing the door open, he jumped to the ground and moved swiftly to where Jenice was sitting on a rock. "Jenice," he smiled. "Is it really you? What are you doing here in a place like this? There must be a story here somewhere. 'Fess up. What is it, gal?"

"Roy Jenkins?" Jenice observed, rising to her feet. Her mind ached, and nothing seemed clear—but Roy Jenkins she recognized. "I— I'm sorry. My mind is a little foggy at the moment. If there's a story I'm not sure what it is."

Roy's smile widened. "Oh yeah, sure. I believe you, gal. I believe you."

Michael stepped forward. "I take it you two know each other," he said.

"We've covered a few stories together," Jenice replied. "Roy's a reporter, too."

"Hey, babe. What's this about we've covered stories together? I'd say our relationship goes a little deeper than that. The time we've spent together off work stays in my mind more than the work time." With no warning, Roy stepped forward and kissed her. "That's what I remember best," he said. "It hurts that you'd remember only the work."

Jenice glanced at Michael. Even in her foggy state, she realized the hurt in his eyes went much deeper than appearances showed. She couldn't deny there had been fun times with Roy, but that was all before she had met Michael. She wanted to say something, but Michael moved so quickly she didn't have the chance.

"Look, Roy," Michael said. "It's obvious you and Jenice are pretty good friends. She has a concussion, a bad one. I trust you'll go with her to a hospital where she can get the help she needs."

"You're the one with the concussion?" Roy asked. "I'm sorry, Jenice. I didn't realize. Yes, yes. I will take care of her . . ."

Roy looked over at Michael, apparently hoping for an introduction. "Name's Michael Allen. Jenice and I are—friends. Here, I'll help you get her to the chopper."

"Good idea, Michael," Roy agreed, taking one side of Jenice while Michael took the other. Together they got her into the craft. In the meantime, Brad help Shannon and Tanielle in on the opposite side. They took the front seat that Roy had vacated, while Jenice sat in back. Roy grabbed his camera and circled the chopper, where he slid in the back next to Jenice. He lay his camera on the floor, holding it steady with his feet.

Jenice looked deep into Michael's eyes. "Please," she said, laying a hand to the side of his face. "When this is over, let's meet someplace. Okay?"

Michael drew in a deep breath and exhaled it loudly. "No, Jenice. I don't think we should. We tried that once before, remember? Let's say our good-byes here."

"Please, Michael. I—"

Michael put a finger to her lips. "No. You're not thinking clearly right now. I'm sure you'll feel much different when you get rid of that headache. It's better that you go your way, and I go mine. I wish you a long and wonderful life, Jenice. May you find all the happiness you want and deserve. And may you find someone worthy to share your happiness with . . ." Michael looked at the man in the seat next to her. " . . . Roy here, or whoever else might turn out to be right for you. Who knows, maybe our paths will cross again someday. But even if they don't, I'll never forget you. I hope you'll never forget me."

With her heart aching even more than her head, Jenice watched as Michael backed away and closed the door. "Take good care of her, Roy," he said. "She's the greatest, you know."

"I know," Roy agreed. "I will take care of her, Michael. You take care of yourself, too."

As the engine revved and the blades gathered speed, Michael ducked and backed away. The chopper lifted off and in an instant was pulling away over the dense growth. Jenice strained to see the last possible glimpse of Michael. How could she have been such a fool as to let him go again? There would never be another chance for the two of them. She just knew it.

* * *

The thump, thump, thump of the helicopter blades faded, and was soon gone—taking with it the one love Michael had ever known. By all odds, this time she was gone forever. Even though Michael was immersed in unspeakable pain, in his heart he knew it was for the best. Jenice could never be his.

Learning of Roy Jenkins had come with surprising impact. Michael had never suspected there was someone in Jenice's life before he came along. He knew of Bruce, of course, but Bruce had entered the picture after that summer in Paris.

Up until now, Michael had been convinced Jenice's rejection of commitment had only to do with her love of being free. Was it possible there was more to her walking out of his life, as she had done, than he suspected? Jenice had never mentioned Roy, or any other man for that matter. But it was evident that Roy had had no reservations about kissing Jenice. And Jenice hadn't resisted.

Michael closed his eyes. Maybe if he closed them tightly enough it would block out all that was wrong. It didn't help, but he kept on trying just the same—until he was interrupted by the sound of Brad's voice.

"I—uh—know how you must feel, Michael. I've been there, done that, and got the scars to prove it. I wish there were something I could say."

Michael forced a smile. "It's okay. I'll get over it in time. What do you say you and I get off this island while the getting's still good?"

"Hold up there, matey," Blake said, before Brad could answer. "There be somethin' more I wishes to do before ye leaves me island, Bradley Douglas. I be thinkin' the two of us will never be settin' eyes on each other again."

Brad looked at his old friend. "You're right about one thing," he conceded. "When I leave this time, I'll probably never be back. My house and everything I have here is bound to be destroyed by the storm. I haven't the heart to start over from scratch, especially with Shannon and Tanielle gone. But there's nothing to keep you from coming with me, Blake. Give up this vigil of yours, and follow me back to my old home. I could use a buddy, and so could you. What do you say, old friend. Will you come with me?"

"No, matey. What ye be askin', I cannot do. I think ye knows why."

"Yeah," Brad sighed. "I figured that's what you'd say, but I had to try."

"Before ye leave, I've a gift for ye, to help get ye started in yer new life."

"A gift? What are you talking about?"

"The gift be hidden in the cave, matey. I can't fetch it with these ghostly hands, so ye'll have to fetch it yerself."

"You want me to go back in the cave? Come on, Blake. Surely after all this time you haven't changed your mind about who gets your map?"

"No matey, it be not the map. That be for Oscar Welborn's blood kin. I've another small treasure in mind for ye. If ye'll be so kind as to crawl into the cave, I'll lead ye to where it be hid."

Brad thought about it only a moment. "You're serious about this, aren't you, Blake?"

"Aye, matey, I be serious."

"What about it, Michael? Do you mind waiting a few more minutes while I see what the captain wants?"

Michael motioned toward the cave's entrance. "Be my guest. I left the flashlight lying just inside."

Kneeling down, Brad worked his way through the small opening. The flashlight was right where Michael said it would be.

"Over here, matey," Blake said, as Brad came to his feet. "The treasure be hid behind this rock, says I."

Brad moved to the rock Blake pointed out. "There be a crevasse in the wall behind the rock, matey. Shove in yer hand and ye'll feel me treasure. I placed it there with me own hands on the last day of me mortal life."

Blake had little trouble spotting the crevasse. Dropping to his knees, he inserted his hand in it. Sure enough he felt something small and solid.

Retrieving it, and holding it under the light, Brad discovered that he was holding a miniature chest, about the size of a small brick. It was gold in color, and had miniature handles on each end like one might expect on a larger chest. It even had a latch holding the lid in place.

"Go ahead, matey," Blake said. "Open it up."

Brad worked at the latch, trying to release it. Three hundred years without use made it difficult, but with a little extra pressure it finally let go. Very slowly, he opened the lid and looked inside. "This is full of coins, Blake," he said. "They look like gold coins."

"Aye, matey. That's what they be. They be the coins Oscar Welborn used to pay me for transportin' the lady to the new world. They be me gift to ye. They be worth less than a fortune, to be sure. But they have value enough to be givin' ye a fresh start in yer new world."

"Blake, are you sure?"

"I be sure, matey. What good be gold coins to this salty old ghost? Just take the coins and be gone, Brad Douglas. The storm be almost here."

By the time Brad had crawled back through the makeshift opening, the first signs of the storm had already appeared. High winds whistled through the overhead trees while dark clouds moved in quickly, filling the sky with rumbling thunder and brilliant bursts of lightning. Large drops of rain came crashing down through leaves and branches, scenting the air with the familiar odor of a jungle rain.

"We better make for the boat fast," Brad shouted over the noise of the wind. "I hope you're not the kind to be bothered with motion sickness, Michael, because we're in for one rough ride."

"Never have been," Michael responded. "And I've been through some pretty rough rides in my time."

In the five minutes it took for them to reach the point where the boat was docked, the rain had turned to a stinging, wind-whipped deluge. They wasted no time in taking cover in the cab of the boat. The sound of the engine roaring to life was music to Michael's ears. Brad switched on the windshield wipers, which were barely able to keep up with the driving rain.

"I'm glad this didn't work out with me alone in the boat," Michael admitted. "Can you really find your way to Saint Thomas in this torrent?"

"I know these waters, and I have my instruments to guide me. I'll get us there, Michael. If I don't, you can sue me, all right?"

Brad lay a hand to the throttle, but before moving it—he took one last look at his friend Captain Blake, who stood a little way off on the rain-soaked shore. As their eyes met for perhaps the last time ever, Brad raised a hand, and gave a slight farewell nod. Blake returned the gesture with a wave of his own. Then Brad shoved the throttle full open, and the boat shot forward into the troubled waters.

CHAPTER 17

Captain Blake stood looking at what was left of the house Brad had built. The storm had done a job on it all right. No one would ever live in this house again. It had been two months now, and the days were growing more and more lonesome for the captain. Funny, in the three hundred years he had been on this island, only the last ten had been spiced with company. He hadn't seemed to notice the lonely days so much before those years with Brad Douglas there to help wend away the long hours. But now—things were different. Now the old sea captain knew the meaning of the word "lonely," and it was a word he was beginning to detest. Even to the point of almost giving up his vigil. Almost—but not quite.

"I've given me word, and me word is . . ." He released a long, lingering sigh. "Me word is harder to keep with each passin' day, Angela Marie. What I wouldn't give to be seein' yer face."

There, in his moment of greatest despair, he stared at the long evening shadows formed by the sinking sun. As he did, something caught his eye. A new shadow moved across his vision. A glance backward revealed its source. It was Samantha Hackett.

Blake removed his hat and held it across his chest. "Excuse me, ma'am. I didn't hear ye coming up behind me." The thought crossed his mind that she, being a ghost like himself, should cast no shadow. For the moment, he shrugged off the idea.

"I know," Samantha replied. "You were so taken up in your thoughts you didn't notice me. I've been watching you for several minutes. You miss him, don't you? Brad, I mean."

"Aye, lassie, it be true. I miss me friend. He be gone for good, ye see. I'll never be castin' me eyes on him again."

Samantha smiled. "Well, Captain Blake, that's not necessarily true. You see, there are some things I know that you don't. Not yet, anyway. But you will before my visit here is finished today. Does this look familiar to you, Captain?" Samantha held up an object for him to see.

Captain Blake's eyes opened wide. "That be me map, lassie. But this be impossible. Ye be a ghost like meself. Ye can't be holdin' me map. Ye be playin' curious tricks on me mind, says I."

Samantha was still smiling. "No, Captain, I'm not playing tricks. You see, the rules have changed. I'm not that sort of ghost anymore. You'll soon find that there are certain things still ahead for you to learn. One of them has to do with progression in the next dimension. I've just moved to a new level. When the time comes, the same thing will happen to you."

"These be things too deep for this poor mind, says I. I'll not be understandin' the change in ye, but I'll accept it. Why be ye here this time, lassie? Have ye found the name ye be searchin' for?"

"Let's put it this way, I've learned a lot since I was here last. Not only have I learned, I've learned from the best. I've been to a personal seminar presented by a group from the ranks of the higher authorities. Wow—what a kick. I've been a teacher myself, but I have to admit these people put me to shame, Blake. One month in their classroom is worth a millennium in one of mine. They even helped me with my research on your case, Captain. Here, let me show you what I was able to come up with."

Samantha reached in her purse and removed a two-page document, which she handed to Blake. He hesitated to take it from her. "How do ye think I can hold yer document in me ghostly hands, lassie?" he asked.

Samantha laughed. "It's all part of my new image," she explained. "I can handle things from any dimension now. This document is one you can hold, Captain. Go ahead, take it."

Blake reached out and took the document. "By thunder, says I, ye be speakin' the truth."

"I want you to read the document, but before you do there's something I should tell you. Your time has come, Captain Blake. The higher authorities have instructed that I'm not to leave this island without you this time."

Blake's left eye narrowed to a squint. "Ye have a black heart, lassie. I trusted ye with me secret on yer promise not to be pressin' me to break me word. I'll not be leavin' this island until me word is kept."

Samantha folded her arms and glared at Blake. "Before you go getting all bent out of shape, take a minute to read the report. You might be surprised."

After three hundred years of waiting, Blake had little hope these papers would hold anything more than another feeble attempt to lure him across the line without a struggle. But just on the chance he might be wrong, he unfolded the document and studied its contents. The more he read, the more interested he became. Samantha wasn't lying; she really had come up with something meaningful in her report. Slowly, he lowered the paper and looked back at Samantha.

"By the stars, lassie, be this a documented fact?" he asked.

"Oh yes, Captain. It's all documented. Now that you've read it, you should understand why I took the time to stop by your cave. I wanted to retrieve your map. Oh, and by the way, while I was in the cave, I took care of another little item of business. You said you didn't like the idea of sharing your tomb with the likes of Baxter? Well, you're not sharing it with him anymore. I had what was left of him dispatched elsewhere. I hope that makes you happy."

"Ye did this for me, lassie?"

"Oh yes, Captain. And I even documented it, if that helps. With the exception of the missing map, your bones are back exactly as they were. So what about it? Will the arrangements described in my report satisfy your promise to Oscar Welborn?"

"Aye, lassie. I be satisfied, though I trusts no one but ye to be takin' care of these things. Ye will be the one, will ye not?"

"You got it, Captain. Your map is in good hands, and I promise your secret will be given to no one but the blood descendant of Oscar Welborn. I'll take care of it all myself. Now, what do you say? Are you ready to go home?"

Blake handed the document back to Samantha, took a deep breath of air, and looked up at the big red ball that was nearly ready to sink from the sky. He broke out into a giant, ghostly smile. "Is Angela Marie waitin' for me?" he asked.

"She is," Samantha answered with a smile to match the captain's. "And so are all the members of your crew. You can't imagine the grandeur of the places you'll be sailing now, Captain Blake. Not just oceans and not just between continents. You'll be sailing across vast galaxies to worlds beyond description. What do you think of that, huh?"

"I think it be grand, lassie. I be fearin' my sailin' days would be over when I reported to the other side."

"No way, Captain. Sailing is what makes you happy, so sailing is what you get over there. That's the way it works, my friend. Now, before I open your door home, I need to ask you one last question. How would you like to see your friend Brad Douglas again?"

"Are you referrin' to when me matey crosses the line hisself?"

"No, Captain. I'm referring to the very near future, while he's still in the flesh. Would you like to see him again."

"Aye, lassie. That would do me heart good, to be seein' Brad Douglas again. Be it possible?"

Samantha folded the document she had shown Blake and slid it into her purse, alongside the captain's map. "Well," she said. "I think it could be arranged. You see, Captain, when I took the job as Special Conditions Coordinator, I inherited Brad's case. It just so happens he's covered by a special contract, and the terms of his contract have been allowed to slip through the cracks. It's up to me to start putting things back in order, and I begin in the very near future. I'll be needing an angel to help out with the case, and since you already know Brad so well . . ."

"Are ye sayin' ye might send me back as an angel to be workin' with me friend, Bradley?"

"That's exactly what I'm saying, Captain. Are you interested in the job?"

"Aye, lassie. Ye can count me in on that one, says I."

"Good, I'll be contacting you. Now, what do you say we take care of a little matter that's been on hold for the last three centuries? Are you ready?"

Captain Blake replaced his hat, straightened his jacket, and stared right in Samantha's eyes. "Aye, lassie. I be ready. But there be one thing I be needin' to know before we go. When ye threatened to send me to the desert, could ye have done that, or were ye bluffin'? I have to be knowin' the truth."

Samantha laughed. "You're a pretty shrewd old captain at that," she admitted. "The truth is, I could send you anywhere I want *now*, but at the time I was still too low on the totem pole to pull strings, like sending you to the Sahara Desert. No, Captain Blake, I couldn't have made good on my threat. But you didn't know that, and look how well things have turned out because of it."

Now it was Blake's turn to laugh. "Ye be a shrewd one yerself, lassie. It be an honor doin' business with ye."

Samantha wasted no more time. With the snap of her finger, a tiny flicker of light appeared from seemingly out of nowhere. As Blake looked on in amazement, it grew in size and in brilliance until it had the appearance of a noonday sun. Little by little, the center of the light opened, revealing a radiant passageway leading off into the distance as far as the eye could see.

"You asked about Angela," Samantha said. "She's waiting for you just on the other side of this door. Are you ready to step through it now?"

Blake took one last look around at his island. Then, straightening the hat back on his head, and throwing his chest forward, he nodded a definite yes. Samantha slid her arm through his, and led the way into the tunnel. In a matter of seconds, Blake's three-hundred-year wait was over as the two of them were engulfed by the light. Somewhere in the distance a bird sang its cheerful song, as the big orange sun sank silently into the horizon.

CHAPTER 18

Jenice Anderson hit the print command for the news report she had just typed on her office computer. As she checked the printer to be sure it had started, the calender at the edge of her desk caught her eye. *November 10th,* she thought. *Why does that date ring a bell?* Then it hit her. *Yes, of course, today is Michael's birthday. I'll be darned, I almost missed it. I wonder where he is now, and what he's doing. Not that it really matters, I suppose.*

It had been a little over two months since the day Jenice left Michael on the island when she was whisked away to the hospital at Key West. A lot had happened in those two months. A lot indeed.

Jenice leaned back in her chair and let the events of the last two months trickle through her mind. The first week held little memory at all, thanks to her concussion. By the second week, things had started back to normal, but even this period was fuzzy. Thank goodness for Roy Jenkins. What would she have done without him there to help her through the ordeal? Good old Roy. It had been great fun, reliving old times with him. Jenice had forgotten how much fun he could be. It had been so easy to rekindle the old flame. A point well taken, considering the ring she now wore on her left hand.

In a way, the whole thing was quite humorous. That is, if anything about being engaged can be considered humorous. Roy had been around a long time and was the first man she had ever given a second look to. Somehow the subject of marriage never came up between them when they were seeing each other the first time around. In time, they just sort of drifted apart. Then, she met Michael, and they spent that wonderful summer together in Paris.

Michael had been the first man to propose to her. Then, there had been Bruce Vincent.

Jenice held up her hand to admire the ring. She had to admit, it couldn't compare with the one Bruce Vincent had given her, but Bruce was one who could afford the finer things in life. Saying "yes" to Bruce would have set her up for a life of pure luxury. But that was crazy. Adventure is what Jenice craved, not living in a fancy house and driving a Mercedes.

She tried to picture in her mind what the ring might have looked like that Michael had intended to give her. Of course, there was no way she would ever know what that one looked like, since Michael himself told her how he threw it into the Yangtze River while in Shanghai, China. Once in awhile she wondered if she had made a mistake not saying "yes" to Michael when she had the chance. No use looking back now, though. Michael was yesterday, and yesterday is gone forever.

That's where the humorous part came in. After coming so close to saying yes to Michael and Bruce, she ended up right where she had begun, with Roy Jenkins. Sometimes she questioned her decision to accept Roy's proposal, but she quickly reminded herself how perfectly suited she and Roy were for each other. They had so much in common, not the least of which was being highly aggressive reporters. That was the final factor that tipped the scales in Roy's favor. Especially when he suggested the two of them work as partners. Even though Jenice had always played the part of a loner, Roy's suggestion had its merits. A reporter's life is an exciting life, and one that means there's always another adventure waiting just around the corner. As partners, they would never have to feel guilty about leaving the other behind to chase after one of those adventures.

Jenice held her hand a little higher, still admiring the ring, when she caught a glimpse of someone behind her. She looked up to see it was a woman. Not just any woman. It looked like—but no—it couldn't be, of course.

"Pardon me for staring," she said apologetically. "It's just that you remind me of someone. The resemblance is uncanny."

Samantha smiled. "Probably more uncanny than you know, Jenice. I *am* that someone I remind you of. To put it in Dr. Seuss' words—'I am Sam. Sam I am.' And just for the record, I've never tasted green eggs and ham."

Jenice stood to face her unexpected guest. "You're Sam?" she asked in amazement. "I must say, you're more beautiful in person than you are in any of the pictures I've seen of you. Even Jason's holograph didn't do you justice. May I ask why you're here? I know I wouldn't rate a visit from you, unless there was a pretty good reason for one."

"You're right, I do have a good reason. Not an easy one to explain, though. Let's just say I'm here to set some things straight that have been too long neglected."

Jenice shook her head. "Sorry, Sam. You left me in the dust on that one."

"Okay, let's put it another way. I'm here to make you an offer I think you're really going to like. But at the same time, what I'm offering won't come without its price."

"Uh, huh," Jenice said laughing softly. "That clears it up. I understand you about as well as I understand Albert Einstein's thing about relativity. Albert was talking about cousins, aunts, long-lost rich uncles, and the like, wasn't he?"

Samantha grinned and picked up the calendar from Jenice's desk. "I'll get straight to the point. I noticed you looking at this calendar just now. So tell me, what is it that's significant about today's date?"

"You picked up that calender," Jenice exclaimed. "Angels aren't supposed to be able to do that, are they?"

"I've had a few changes in my life lately, Jenice. It's a long story, but I can do things now that I couldn't do before. Like picking up this calendar, for instance. So tell me about it? Why do you have today's date marked in red?"

"I think you know the answer to that, Sam. It's your brother's birthday."

"Okay, what about this date?" Samantha asked, flipping the pages of the calender backward to May 29.

Jenice didn't hesitate with her answer. "That's my mother's birthday," she said.

"Right on, Jenice. You did remember to call your mother on her birthday, didn't you?"

"Sam! What are you getting at?"

"I'm getting to the fact that your mother was born on May 29, 1953. The same day a major event took place in history."

"Are you talking about Mount Everest?" Jenice asked.

"Bingo! That's the day Tenzing Norgay and Edmund Hillary reached the top of the world, the first ever to make it. I happen to know it's always been your dream to stand where they stood, Jenice. You won't deny that, will you?"

"Deny it? Not hardly. I'd give away my birthday for the chance. It was my mother's dream before me, but she married my father instead."

"Now we're getting to my point, Jenice," Samantha said, returning the calender to the desk and picking up a picture. "Is this a picture of your parents?" she asked.

Jenice nodded yes.

"They look happy enough. Does your mother resent your father because marrying him required her to give up her dream?"

"I think I see where you're going with this," Jenice said. "No, my mother never has held it against my father. They're very much in love, and you're right—they are very happy. I'm the one who was always bothered because my mother gave up her dreams. And by dreams I mean more than scaling Mount Everest. My mother was like me, craving a new adventure constantly. And yes, that is the reason I've always had a problem giving in to the idea of marriage. That is what you're getting at isn't it, Sam?"

"I see you're wearing an engagement ring now. How do you explain that, Jenice?"

Jenice looked at the ring. "Roy is different; he's a lot like me. Marrying Roy wouldn't mean giving up my dreams; it would only mean sharing them."

Samantha snickered. "Good old Roy Jenkins, boy reporter to the rescue, so to speak. What about Michael? He's another one who loves one adventure after another, Jenice. I should know. He's my brother and I grew up with him."

"Oh, that's what this is all about. You blame me for hurting your brother."

"I can't deny I was a little bent out of shape when I learned how you walked out on him. And—maybe I still resent it a little bit. Well, maybe more than just a little bit. You did do the same thing to Bruce, you know."

Jenice took the picture from Samantha and replaced it on her desk. "So you're here to lecture me on my insensitivity, is that it?"

"No, Jenice, that's not why I'm here. But part of my reason for being here is to get you to take a real good look at yourself. I'm going to get personal, and I doubt if you'll like it much—but I'm left with little choice since I've inherited the responsibility for setting your destiny back on its designated course. And if all this seems hard for you to understand, just try thinking of me as your newly appointed guardian angel, okay?"

"My guardian angel? That's a little trite, wouldn't you say, Sam."

"It is not trite. Everyone has angels looking out for them. Granted, on my side we don't refer to them as guardian angels, but it's close enough if it helps you understand why I'm here. Now, let me ask you again; why do you feel comfortable marrying Roy and not Michael, even knowing that Michael loves adventure as much as you do?"

"I guess you deserve an answer to your question since he is your brother. Michael does love adventure, but he also loves to paint. Painting is more than just a hobby with him; painting is his way of earning a living. I'm a reporter, and as a reporter I have to be ready to head off somewhere at the sound of the phone. Roy happens to be a reporter, too—"

Samantha cut in. "So you and Roy would both be ready to go at the sound of the same phone call."

"That's right, Sam. Michael and I wouldn't share that luxury. In fact, that's the very reason I couldn't meet him at the Eiffel Tower." Jenice looked straight at Samantha. "You do know about that, I assume?"

Samantha didn't bother answering Jenice's question. Instead, she asked a question of her own. "Do you love Roy Jenkins, Jenice?"

"Love him?" Jenice asked. "Quite frankly, I don't see how that's any of your business, Sam."

"Like I said, Jenice. Much about you is my business now. I'm not backing off 'til I get an answer. Do you love Roy Jenkins?"

Jenice felt her blood pressure jump a count or two. If this were just a woman pressing her for something so personal, she'd tell her where to get off pretty darn quick. But Samantha was anything but "just a woman." Not only was she Michael Allen's sister, she was also an angel. A pushy angel, yes, but an angel, nevertheless. Jenice contained her anger, and just answered the question. "I'm not sure what I feel for Roy is real love. I am very fond of him, and he is good to me."

Samantha broke out with a hearty laugh. "Talk about coming full circle," she said. "This conversation reminds me of one I had with a fellow named Gus, when I was considering marrying Bruce Vincent. You're fond of him, you say? How about Michael? Are you fond of him, too?"

The question hit Jenice like a dagger to the heart as her mind's eye drew a picture of Michael's face. "I—I'm more than fond of Michael," she painfully conceded. "I admit that. But even if I did have second thoughts about Michael, it's a little too late for me. Michael's made it pretty clear he could never trust me again. I can't say that I blame him. What I did was pretty rotten."

"I'll go along with the rotten part, but you're wrong about the rest. To be perfectly honest, I wish Michael wasn't in love with you, but . . ." Samantha shrugged. "I learned a long time ago I can't do Michael's thinking for him. You could have him back in a heartbeat if you'd stop listening to that stubborn streak of yours and tell him how much you love him. That's something you never have told him, you know."

"I know. That's something I've never said to any man, my father included. I don't even know why. It's just something I can't get out."

Samantha threw up her hands. "What is this?" she moaned. "You're making all the same mistakes I made with Jason. It's funny how different things look from the other side of the fence. But—let's get back to the subject at hand—your dreams."

Samantha reached for the keyboard on Jenice's computer. Pulling it in front of her, she typed in a quick command. Jenice couldn't believe her eyes. A picture of Mount Everest came up on the screen, and not just any picture. The picture vividly depicted a mountain storm with huge wind-blown flakes of snow blowing violently about. The chilling sound of the wind could even be heard.

"This is impossible," Jenice gasped. "I have nothing like that loaded on my computer. How did you do that, Sam?"

Samantha grinned, and proceeded to look very knowledgeable. "Doing the impossible is so easy anymore, sometimes I just can't resist. Wait 'til you see what I have planned next."

Samantha reached into her purse and removed a large white envelope, which she handed to Jenice. "Here, take a look at this."

Jenice took the envelope, but she didn't open it. "What is it?" she asked, looking the outside over carefully.

Samantha smiled. "Offhand," she answered frankly, "I'd call it a dream. Go ahead, Jenice, open it and see for yourself."

"A dream? I hope you don't mind me being skeptical, Sam. But I've found when someone hands me something they call a dream, what's inside is usually a pretty big disappointment."

"Not so in this case, Jenice. It's a dream all right. Not my dream, but yours. The same one you're looking at on your computer screen."

Jenice raised a hand to her chin. "You're playing games with me, Sam. What does this envelope have to do with Mount Everest?"

"It has everything to do with Mount Everest, that is if you're telling the truth about wanting to climb the darn thing. That envelope holds your ticket, Jenice. If you decide to accept it, that is."

Jenice was more skeptical than ever. "Are you trying to say you've set me up for a climbing expedition to scale Mount Everest?"

"You'll have to furnish your own ski mask and parka, but the rest is on me."

Slowly, Jenice opened the envelope and took out an official-looking contract. Glancing it over quickly, she realized it was a contract guaranteeing her place on an upcoming expedition. It even had places for both her and Samantha to sign. "Is this for real, Sam?" she asked after a close examination of the contract.

"It's for real, Jenice. Sign your name on the bottom line, and the expedition is yours."

"I don't know what to say, Sam. This is all so overwhelming. There has to be a catch. There is a catch, isn't there?"

"The contract doesn't come without a price, if that's what you mean, Jenice. It's all there in bold print. Sign the dotted line, and you have yourself a dream come true. But if you do, you have to sign away your right to even so much as speak to my brother again. You said that Michael doesn't trust you. Well, neither do I, Jenice. I know you love him, and I know he loves you. But you left him standing in the rain at the Eiffel Tower just for the fun of flying a Russian jet.

"I'm willing to offer my assistance in getting the two of you back together, but only if you prove you can be trusted this time. As you can see, I deliberately made the stakes higher than a ride in a jet. And I'm giving you about the same amount of time you had to make your decision in Paris. You have five minutes. The clock is rolling and the seconds are ticking off. The choice is yours, Jenice. Michael, or the dream of climbing to the highest point in the world."

* * *

As he stood on the thick, green carpet of hybrid grass bordering the main entrance to the city museum, Jason wondered how he had ever gotten himself into a situation like this. Was it barely two months ago that he had been the head chef at the Paradise Palace? Jason had loved being a chef. How had he ever gotten tangled up with this Special Conditions Coordinator thing anyway? As far as he was concerned, Gus had been doing a great job. Why couldn't things have just stayed the way they were? One thing he vowed, and that was never to type out a contract by himself. Not after the mess Gus had made with his infamous typo.

Jason glanced up at the clear blue sky. Not one cloud in sight. He knew what he had to do; he just wasn't sure if he really knew how. Over the years, he had watched Gus do things like control the weather on several occasions. But that was Gus. Gus was supposed to be able to do things like that.

Jason also knew there wasn't much time for lingering. Samantha was already with Jenice, taking care of her part of the plan—a plan Samantha had put together with Jason's help. Well, Jason had sort of helped put it together. He did come up with the part about retrieving the ring from the Yangtze River. A nice touch, if he did say so himself.

Once again, he glanced upward at the sky. Taking a deep breath and pointing a finger high above his head, he did exactly as he had been taught in Special Conditions Coordinator school. To his utter amazement, lightning flashed and thunder rolled on the edge of the sky. From out of seemingly nowhere, dark clouds appeared and began moving rapidly in the direction of the museum.

"WOW!" he exclaimed, looking at the end of his finger. "IT WORKED! I DID IT! I REALLY DID IT!"

There he stood in near disbelief, watching the gathering clouds grow thicker and thicker as they moved ever nearer. "Well," he said, smiling to himself. "Now that I've taken care of the weather, I'd better get inside. Samantha's brother is waiting for me, and I have more work to do."

By this time, the clouds had reached a point in the sky where they moved past the midday sun, shadowing the world below with a thick blanket of darkness. Jason shivered with excitement. "This Special Conditions Coordinator thing isn't so bad," he said grinning like a boy flying his first kite. "I just might like this change after all. Especially since I can open my own door on the way into the museum."

* * *

"You're down to under three minutes, Jenice," Samantha said, with a deliberate sting in her voice. "You haven't signed your name yet. That dream of yours is sprouting wings, and they're growing bigger by the second."

Jenice rested the tip of her pen on the dotted line. Why couldn't she make her hand move? One signature and a lifetime's dream was hers, guaranteed by an angel, for crying out loud. What possible difference could it make if she never saw Michael again? She was planning to marry Roy, anyway. But until now, pushing Michael outside the circle of her life had never seemed this real. It was just sort of an abstract thing, like seeing Tom Cruise shot and killed in one movie, only to see him very much alive and kicking in his next release. The pressure was just too much for her to handle.

"Please, Sam. Give me more time. I need a little more time."

"All right," Samantha unexpectedly agreed. "Just to show you I do have a heart, I'll put the clock on hold at one minute and thirteen seconds. But I'm leaving it on hold just long enough to tell you a little story about myself when I was faced with choosing between Bruce and Jason. You see, Jenice, my story is not unlike your own. Like you and Roy, Bruce and I had something in common. We were both alive. And like Michael and you, Jason and I had a huge barrier between us. He lived in his dimension, and I lived in mine.

"At the time of my greatest turmoil, a special person came to my apartment to see me. His name was Gus Winkelbury. First, he asked me how I felt about Bruce. I explained my feelings about the same way you explained yours when I asked about Roy. Then, in that crazy accent of his, Gus asked a question that almost tore my heart out. He said, 'Tell me this, Sam. If yer only fond of Bruce, how do ya feel about Jason?' When I didn't give him a straight answer, he asked another question. 'How would ya feel if he never came here ta see ya again?' That question got my attention, Jenice. Like I got yours by offering a trip up the mountain if you agreed never to see Michael again. Gus said something like this:

'I want ya ta think about this, Sam. No one but you can make the choice between Bruce and Jason. Just remember that choice comes with some good, and some bad. Ya can't have it all. If ya choose Bruce, Jason will be gone for good. And it works the other way, too. Ya can't have them both, so think hard on it before makin' the choice.'

"Gus was saying that either decision I made would bring up a problem or two. Now it's my turn to pass that little seed of wisdom along to you, Jenice. Either way you go will bring problems. If you choose Roy and the mountain, Michael will be gone forever. If you choose Michael, there will always be the problem of the difference in your lifestyles, just like any two people might have to face. Your parents, for instance. In their case, they faced the problems and moved on. In your case, it might even mean giving up your job as a reporter. That's a very real possibility, and one you should face up front.

"Now that I have everything painted jet black, let me play Paul Harvey and tell 'the rest of the story.' When I chose Jason, I had to give up a lot more than a trip up a mountain. My choice cost me fifty some odd years of life on this side. At the time, that seemed like a pretty big sacrifice. I was wrong. As it worked out, it was no sacrifice at all. The world I live in now makes this one look pretty bare and simple. And best of all, I have my Jason. Where would I be now if I'd chosen Bruce? Living out a lie with a man I didn't really love, that's where.

"Oh, and one thing more. I know you don't fully understand it just yet, but there happens to be a forever contract binding your destiny to Michael's. Not that you have to honor that contract; you can say no to it. But if you do, your destiny will never be fulfilled. I can guarantee you'll live to rue the day you turned it down. That's all

I have to say, Jenice. The rest is up to you. Your clock is running. You have one minute and thirteen seconds to decide."

Try as she would, Jenice couldn't force the picture of Michael from her mind. In desperation, she looked at the computer screen hoping the mountain scene would help straighten her thoughts. But—instead of Mount Everest—the screen was now filled with an image of Michael's face. In one last desperate attempt at claiming her dream, Jenice put the pen against the paper.

"Thirty seconds," she heard Samantha say. "Twenty-five.

Fifteen. Going . . . going . . ."

Tightening her fist around the pen, Jenice whirled and threw it across the room. "You win, Sam!" she shouted. "I'm in love with your brother! Is that what you wanted to hear me say? Forget my dream. If there's a chance you can get the two of us back together, then do your thing, all right?"

It was impossible for Jenice to discern whether Samantha's sigh was one of relief or disappointment, but it really didn't matter at the moment. Taking the contract in both hands, Jenice ripped it in half and tossed it in her waste basket. "I hope you know, Sam, that was not an easy thing for me to do," she said.

Samantha looked at the torn paper at the bottom of Jenice's waste basket. "I didn't mean for it to be easy," she countered. "Now I know I can trust you with my brother's heart. I was pretty sure you'd come through, that's why I asked Jason to help me out. Michael doesn't know it, but Jason is with him. Right about now they should be standing in the rain in front of the Eiffel Tower."

"In front of the Eiffel Tower?" Jenice gasped. "Michael is back in Paris?"

"Well, not exactly," Samantha admitted. "But close enough. If Jason did everything I asked him to do, Michael will be pretty well softened up by now. All we have to do is get you there so you can deliver the knockout punch."

Samantha reached in her purse again. This time she pulled out a small shiny object which she handed to Jenice. "You'll need this," she said.

Jenice took the object and examined it. "A ring?" she asked. "I don't get it."

"What's to get? Michael puts the ring on your finger and presto you're engaged. Just like you did with Bruce and Roy. Only this time, the ring stays. Otherwise, you are going to face the wrath of one very angry angel."

Jenice shook her head. "Is it some sort of tradition in your family for the sister to furnish her brother with a ring?"

"I'm not furnishing the ring, Jenice. This is the same ring Michael bought in Paris. You know, the one you could have had if—"

"If I'd shown up for our rendezvous," Jenice interrupted. "Do you have any idea how tired I am of hearing that? But how can this be the ring? Michael told me himself he—"

This time Samantha interrupted. "He told you how he threw the ring into the Yangtze River. And yes, I know what you're thinking. That it's not possible. But you have to understand, finding something the size of this ring in the Yangtze River is a snap for a talented Special Conditions Coordinator like me." Samantha caught a quick breath. "My gosh," she gasped. "I'm starting to sound just like Gus. What a frightening thought."

Jenice was dumbfounded. "This is the same ring Michael threw in the river? And you found it again? This boggles my mind, Sam. You really could have worked me into an excursion up the side of Mount Everest, couldn't you?"

"I could have, yes. But you showed enough good sense to keep me from having to. Now, are you ready to get a little wet, Jenice? Jason has a nice little rainstorm all prepared."

"Rainstorm? You mentioned something about Michael standing in the rain. Are you taking me to him?"

"That's the general plan. You're not objecting, are you?"

"No, but what do I do when we get there? The last time I saw Michael, he was anything but receptive to me."

"Tell him you love him, Jenice. Jason has him softened up, but getting him to put that ring on your finger is up to you. Now, reach out and touch my hand, and get ready for the trip of your life."

Jenice appeared shocked. "The trip of my life? I take it we're not going by car?"

"Not this time, Jenice. I'll be sending you by direct wire, so to speak. And by the way, I won't be with you. The last thing you need is Michael's big sister looking over your shoulder."

Jenice hesitated. "Will I ever see you again, Sam?" she asked.

"You never can tell," Samantha laughed. "I do some pretty unpredictable things at times. I might drop in when you least expect me. I will be at the wedding. You can take that to the bank. But I probably won't show myself. It's your day, Jenice, not mine. I wouldn't do anything to spoil it, not for the world. Not even for the whole universe, for that matter," she added with a shrug.

"I—have a question, Sam. Do you mind my being candid?"

"Not at all. Let's hear it."

Jenice cleared her throat. "You don't like me very well do you? I mean, the way I treated your brother and your good friend, Bruce . . ."

Samantha smiled. Then taking a step forward, she pulled Jenice into a hug. "I confess," she said. "I didn't like you in the beginning. That was mostly because I was judging you by your sister, Rebecca. But I was wrong, Jenice. You're quite a lady. I'll count it an honor having you for my sister."

"You were judging me by Rebecca?" Jenice gasped. "That's not fair, Sam. I'm nothing like Rebecca. She's a snob."

Samantha laughed. "More of an arrogant snob, I'd say. And she sure can't cook roast duck."

"Roast duck? She can't boil water without burning it. And she has the manners of a pit bull," Jenice laughingly added.

"You shouldn't say that, Jenice. I've known some pretty nice pit bulls."

By this time both were laughing so hard they had tears rolling down their faces. Jenice pulled Samantha back into a hug. "Thanks for the nice things you said about me, Sam," she sniffed. "The feeling goes both ways, you know." She laughed again. "I think we both agree I could use a new sister."

Samantha stepped back and wiped her eyes. "Michael is one lucky man," she said. "You're the best thing ever to happen to him, Jenice. I know I'll be leaving him in good hands. And speaking of hands, it's time you touched mine. You have a long overdue appointment waiting out there in the rain."

CHAPTER 19

Michael punched his time ticket and placed it in the "out" slot. This would be the last time. Working as a museum security guard had been good, as nine to five jobs go, but a year and a half is long enough to stay with any nine-to-five job. Michael's first love was painting. But painting was impossible when every time his brush touched the canvas, only one subject came to mind—her face.

In some ways, running into Jenice again had been good. At least now, there was some semblance of closure to that chapter of his life. Especially after Roy Jenkins had walked into the picture.

Michael still wasn't certain how all the strange circumstances came about that had brought Jenice and him together for one eventful day on a Caribbean island. There were too many loose ends involved to credit it to coincidence. But, whatever the cause and reason, it was over now. Through all his hurt, Michael realized the time had come for him to face life and get back into the race. That meant returning to his first love, painting.

Glancing out the window, Michael was surprised to see it was raining. Strange . . . the last time he looked, it appeared to be a bright, sunny day. He laughed to himself. Maybe some of those strange events, like the ones in the Caribbean, were at it again. Little did he realize just how close to the truth he was with this deduction.

Since Jason chose to remain invisible, Michael had no way of knowing he wasn't alone. Nor did he suspect some of the thoughts popping into his mind were the result of the subliminal suggestions of his unseen guest.

Michael took his coat and favorite Indiana Jones hat from his otherwise empty locker. Here was another curious point: why had he worn the coat and hat to work that morning? It was almost as if a little voice had warned him he would need them before the day was over. Now it was raining and, sure enough, he did need them. He shrugged off the thought, and put on the coat and hat.

Pushing his way through the revolving glass doors, he stepped into the rain and began leisurely walking along the sidewalk that paralleled the museum. Michael didn't own a car; he usually took the bus. This time, however, he decided to walk. His apartment was only a few blocks away, and a walk in the rain just seemed to fit the pattern of his already melancholy mood. After only a couple of steps, something in the museum display window caught his eye. It was the painting of Jenice, the one he had donated to the museum when he first came here.

For some reason, Michael felt particularly drawn to the picture today, which was strange, since he hardly ever looked at it anymore. It depicted the Eiffel Tower, with Jenice in the foreground, and was the last canvas he had painted.

Michael moved closer to the display window. There he stood, doing the very thing he had vowed not to do, reminiscing all over again. Nothing he could do would drive these thoughts from his mind. It was as though he was there again, at the Eiffel Tower. Everything, the sound and smell of a falling rain, the feel of its chill against his face, the ache that refused to leave his heart, all were exactly the same as the day he waited in vain for Jenice to come to him. Pulling his collar tight against his neck, he gave way to the persistent memories as they easily overflowed the dam of indifference he had so carefully attempted to construct in his mind. He remembered, and he died a little. It was impossible to tell whether his eyes were dampest from the outside rain, or from the pain inside his heart.

Then, something else caught his attention. It wasn't enough that he was drawn so powerfully to the picture of Jenice in the painting, now his imagination had conjured up her image as a reflection in the display window. The details of his imaginary reflection were real beyond belief. She was wearing a rain-soaked red dress with matching red pumps, but no jacket. Her makeup was a streaked mess, and her hair was soaked. A rain-drenched purse hung limply off one shoulder. She looked a mess. She looked a terrible mess. But never had she look more beautiful.

Michael was afraid that if he moved, she would vanish altogether. He stood there mesmerized by the reflection—until she spoke his name.

"Hello, Michael. It's a little wet to be standing here looking at a picture of the Eiffel Tower, wouldn't you say?"

Michael spun to face her. "Jenice?" he gasped, unable to take his eyes off her. "Is it you, or is it . . ."

"It's me, Michael." She reached out and lay her hand against his face. "If I were a dream, you wouldn't feel my hand, would you?"

"But where did you—why would you . . .?"

"I'm here to wish you a happy birthday, Michael. That, and to keep an appointment. I'm a little late, I admit. But other than that, everything's pretty much as it should be. We have the rain, and even the Eiffel Tower, if we count your painting."

Michael lay his hand atop hers. "But—how did you know where to find me?"

Jenice's eyes closed tightly, and her lower lip started to quiver. She swallowed hard, drew a quick breath, then managed to force her eyes open. "Your sister brought me here," she choked out. "She's really a wonderful person when you give her the chance."

"My sister? Are you telling me . . . ?"

"I'm telling you Samantha came to me. We had a great talk and—"

"You've seen Sam?" Michael blurted out. "You talked with her?"

"Oh boy, did we talk," she said, brushing her free hand across her eyes. "She told me you still love me. And she brought me here."

Jenice removed a shaky right hand from Michael's face and reached into her purse. Pulling out the ring Samantha had given her, she showed it to Michael. "She gave me this. Do you know what it is, Michael?"

Michael took the ring from her and examined it. "It looks like—no—it can't be. There's no way."

"You're wrong, Michael. It is the ring you wanted to give me in Paris. Crazy as it sounds, your sister managed to retrieve it from the bottom of the Yangtze River . . . I never got to see the ring last time. It's beautiful. You have great taste."

Suddenly, Jenice caught a glimpse of the other ring, still on the finger of her left hand. The ring Roy had given her. She had forgotten to remove it. Instantly, both hands shot behind her back in an effort to take it off before Michael could notice.

"What is it?" Michael asked.

"Uh—it's nothing," she stammered, trying desperately to remove the stubborn ring that refused to budge.

"No really," Michael insisted. "Something's wrong. Is it me? Did I say something . . . ?"

"No, Michael, you've done nothing wrong," she said through clenched teeth as she frantically fought to get the ring off her finger. Then, just when it seemed there was no way she could get the ring off unnoticed, something happened. With no apparent explanation, the ring suddenly expanded until it literally fell off her finger. Jenice closed her hand tightly around it, and did her best to give the appearance that everything was fine. She even managed a smile, as she dropped the ring into her purse without Michael appearing to notice.

"Wow," she said looking right at Michael. "That sister of yours really is something else."

"Sam was—that is, she is—quite a woman," Michael agreed, having no idea what had prompted Jenice's remark.

The two were silent for several seconds. Jenice finally spoke. "So here I am, Michael. Standing in the rain, in front of your rendition of the Eiffel Tower. Is there something you'd like to say to me? Maybe ask me?"

Michael looked back at the ring he was holding. None of this made any sense. How could Sam have found the ring? Angels were certainly capable of doing things mortals could never dream of doing, he concluded. And for that matter, how had she brought Jenice here? Then it hit him. The rain, the picture of the Eiffel Tower. She was doing it again. Even as an angel, Samantha was meddling in his love life. When he was a teenager, she used to set him up with one date after another. She especially did her best to get him and Arline Wilson together. Even though there was no chemistry between Arline and Michael, she refused to let it go easily. Michael laughed inside. Now Arline was married to Bruce Vincent, the very man Samantha was engaged to when the accident took her.

Another thought came to Michael. *You don't suppose? Yes! That sister of mine must have played Cupid from her side to get Bruce and Arline together. I'm on to you, Sam. You're trying to do the same thing to me, aren't you?*

"Darn you, Michael Allen," Jenice scolded when he didn't take her first hint. "Put that blasted ring on my finger so we can get out of this rain. I turned down a lifetime dream to be here for this moment."

Michael eyed Jenice. "Do you know how ridiculous you look standing there drenched like a drowning cat?" he asked. "Pretty darn ridiculous, I'd say." Michael's eyes softened. "Pretty darn beautiful, too," he added, his finger lightly touching her lips.

"Let me see if I have this straight. You refuse to meet me in front of the real Eiffel Tower, but you have come here to the museum to meet me in front of this painting. And you're asking me to go through with what I had intended for the real rendezvous? You're crazy, Jenice Anderson. You're crazy, you're soaking wet, you're beautiful . . ." He paused briefly before adding, "And I love you."

Jenice was crying again, harder this time. "All right, so I didn't make the original rainy day in front of the real Eiffel Tower. I never said I was perfect. Are you going to put that ring on my finger, or not?"

Michael looked deeper into her eyes, but didn't budge. "Say it," he murmured softly.

Jenice remained hypnotized by his eyes. "I—did say it, Michael. Put the ring on my finger."

Michael didn't budge. "Say it!" he came back, much stronger this time.

Jenice squirmed nervously. "What is it you want me to say?" she asked, trying to sound innocent.

"Say it, Jenice. I've waited long enough to hear those words that you can't seem to get past your lips. Now say it!"

Jenice shifted her weight nervously from one foot to the other. "I—I . . ."

"Saaay it . . ."

"All right," she blurted out, her eyes wetter with tears than from the rain. "I love you! Now will you please put that ring on my finger?"

Michael grinned the grin of a happy man. He took Jenice's left hand and placed the ring on the very tip of her finger. There he stopped. "Just one more question, Jenice. Are you doing this because it's your idea—or did that pushy sister of mine put you up to it?"

Jenice shoved her finger through the ring, then throwing both arms around Michael's neck—kissed him like all the world depended on it. Who knows? Maybe it did.

* * *

"All right!" Samantha squealed, giving Jason a kiss of his own. "We did pretty darn good on our first assignment together in our new job, didn't we, my cute little Special Conditions Coordinator?"

Jason scratched the back of his head. "I just don't understand you, Sam. I don't understand you at all. You have no use for Jenice Anderson, and yet when your brother asks her to marry him you flip out. I don't get it."

Both of Samantha's hands flew to her hips. "What is it with you, Jason Hackett? What would ever possess you to say a thing like that? I love Jenice Anderson. She's a wonderful woman, and she's perfect for Michael. I couldn't have picked him a better wife myself."

"But, Sam, you said—"

Samantha broke out laughing and kissed Jason again. "Just because I'm a big shot coordinator doesn't take away from the fact that I'm still a woman. I can change my mind if I want to."

Jason just stared at her. "If you think so highly of Jenice, why did you dangle her dream in front of her face, and then take it away? That wasn't very nice, you know. I know what you were doing—you were testing her to see if she'd choose Michael over her dream. But she did it, Sam. Why not let her have her adventure, too?"

"Jason, Jason, Jason. I'm surprised at how you underestimate me, even after all this time. I have a better adventure in mind for Jenice than climbing some stupid mountain. What I have in mind is an adventure to end all adventures, and one she can share with my brother. I've never told you how I managed to get Captain Blake across the line, have I?"

"No you haven't, Sam. And I've wondered about that."

"It was easy. First, I tricked him into telling me the whole story of why he refused to go home. Next I did some digging on my own. I even asked the higher authorities for help, which they were glad to give. I learned even more of the story than Blake knew himself. You see, Oscar Welborn was dying when he sent his cargo on that fatal voyage with Captain Blake and his crew. Oscar knew he was dying, but he kept it to himself. He did die, too. In fact, he was dead even before Captain Blake."

Jason shrugged. "That's interesting, Sam. But I don't see what it has to do with anything. Blake would have been just as stubborn about getting the map in the hands of Oscar's descendant regardless of all that."

"That's true. So I searched a few files and found out who one of Oscar's descendants is. Bet you'll never guess, Jason."

"I give up, Sam. Who is he?"

Samantha's grin expanded to fill her whole face. "You're looking at him, my cute little Special Conditions Coordinator. In fact, *he* just kissed you not two minutes ago."

"What? You, Sam?"

"Oh yes, I'm a true descendant of Oscar, all right. I had no trouble at all convincing Blake to cross the line once he realized it."

"Now wait a minute, Sam. Blake was looking for a *living* descendant of Oscar Welborn. Granted, you're a living descendant but not in the sense Blake had in mind."

"No—I'm not. But *he* is." Samantha pointed to her brother Michael, who had finally broken off kissing Jenice and was now placing his coat around her. "I made a deal with the captain. He would cross the line, and I'd get the map to my brother. Which I did, by the way. It's in his jacket pocket, along with a note of explanation telling exactly what Captain Blake's lady is all about."

"So do you mind telling me what the lady is? Or is that right reserved for your brother alone?"

"I can tell you now. I promised not to say a word to anyone before getting the map to Michael. Remember how I told you Oscar Welborn was dying. Well, Oscar had a son living in the new world with his wife and family. It was only natural for Oscar to want to leave his wealth to his son. So, he sent the lady by way of Captain Blake's ship. Poor Oscar had no way of knowing the ship would hit a storm and sink."

"All right, Sam. Get to the point. What the heck is the lady? A mummy?"

"No, Jason. Use your head. Captain Blake was the only person Oscar trusted to know the truth. Between the two of them they came up with the idea of calling it the lady. Actually, Oscar put his entire wealth into gold bars. That's what the lady is—a trunk of gold bars that was on its way to Oscar's only son. And that's why I say Jenice is going to get her adventure. What do you think she and my brother will do when they learn about this?"

Jason laughed, then he pulled Samantha into his arms. "And you plan on helping them retrieve the gold off the bottom of the Atlantic, don't you?"

"Maybe," Sam answered elusively. "First I have to help straighten out Brad Douglas' life, then— who knows?"

"You know what, Mrs. Hackett?" Jason asked, looking into her big, bright, sky-blue eyes.

"No, Mr. Hackett, what?"

"I love you, that's what." With that, he kissed her. Their lips parted and Jason ran his fingers through her silky blond hair. "Now," he said, with a smile bigger than the Milky Way. "Isn't there one more thing for you to do before we leave?"

Samantha returned his smile. "There is," she affirmed. "And this is the part I'm going to enjoy the most."

"So will your brother," Jason replied. "So will your brother."

* * *

Arm in arm, Jenice and Michael walked through the rain—going no place in particular. Jenice lay her head on his shoulder and looked at the ring on her finger. "Where do you suppose we'd be right now if I'd accepted this the first time around?" she asked.

"Who cares," Michael answered. "You accepted it now. That's all that matters. Tell me something. When you saw Sam, did she look— you know . . ."

"Did she look happy, you mean?"

"Yeah, that's what I mean. I know she's an angel and all, but . . ."

"You can put your mind at ease, Michael Allen. From what I saw she couldn't be happier."

Michael sighed. "I've never forgiven myself for missing her

funeral, Jenice. It's great knowing you've seen her, and that she's happy. It would have been nice, though, if I could have . . ."

"Seen her yourself?" came a voice from behind. "Turn around, little brother. You might just get your wish."

Michael whirled around. "Sam!" he cried out at the sight of her. "It is you! You—you look . . ."

"I look great, right?" Samantha teased.

"Yes! You look great!"

"And to answer your question, yes, I did play Cupid between you and Jenice. Just like always, you were too darned blind and stubborn to know what was best for you, so I had to step in. That's what big sisters are for. And you listen to me, Michael. Jenice Anderson is one fine lady. You take good care of her, you hear?"

Michael was too choked up to even venture an answer. He swallowed and looked at Jenice, who smiled and gave him a gentle nudge toward Sam. "Go to her, Michael," Jenice urged. "She's the only woman I don't mind sharing you with."

Michael moved to within inches of his sister. There the two of them stood looking at each other. "Can I—that is, I know you're an angel—"

"I'm a second level angel now, Michael. I can do things I couldn't before—and that includes a hug for my little brother." She opened her arms and they hugged. They hugged, and they cried. "Tell Mom and Dad I love them and that I'm all right, will you, Michael?"

"I'll tell them."

"And say hi to Bruce and Arline for me while you're at it, okay?"

"I'll do that, too, Sam."

"And get inside out of this rain before you catch cold."

Michael held her all the tighter. "That's my sister," he choked out. "I love you, Sam."

Samantha backed away a step. "I love you too, Michael." Then brushing away a tear and smiling, she added, "I have to be going. I'm a very important person on the other side now, you see. They can't get along without me for long."

Michael raised his hand in a soft wave. "Thanks, Sam. And good-bye."

"Good-bye, little brother. Take good care of Jenice or I may be back to haunt you."

Jenice stepped close to Michael and slid her arm through his. Together they watched as Samantha slowly faded from their sight. "I'm glad you got to see her," Jenice whispered to Michael.

"Yeah," he answered, still staring at the point where he had last seen her. "So am I."

Jenice slipped her hand into the pocket of Michael's jacket that he had wrapped around her, and felt something there. "What's this?" she asked, pulling out a leather pouch with a folded note attached to it.

"I have no idea," Michael shrugged. "I never saw it before. Tell you what, let's stop in that little French cafe and have something warm. We can look over the pouch there."

"Good idea," Jenice agreed. "I'm starved."

As they made their way across the street to the small cafe, Jenice stumbled slightly and Michael tightened his grip on her arm protectively. Neither of them noticed that Roy's ring had slipped out of Jenice's purse, landing on the rain-soaked sidewalk a short distance away.

Though unseen to this world, Samantha and Jason were still nearby watching. Samantha walked over and picked up the ring. "I'm getting pretty good at retrieving these things," she laughed. "I'll figure a way of getting this one back to Roy. Who knows, maybe I can even find a sweet young finger for him to slide it on."

"Sam!" Jason fussed. "I was hoping you'd give some of this up now that you're a Special Conditions Coordinator. It is a respectable position, you know."

Samantha slid her arm through Jason's and lay her head on his shoulder. "Admit it, Jason. You wouldn't want me to change one little bit." She rolled her eyes and looked teasingly into his. "Would you?"

"Well—do I have to answer that right now, or can I think it over first?"

The rain continued to fall, as though washing away yesterday's mistakes—and offering the promise of a brand new tomorrow for all who would reach out and take it.

ABOUT THE AUTHOR

Dan Yates is a strong believer in the power of storytelling. "It is my belief that using a story for teaching is the best way possible to get a point across. I learned this principle from the greatest teacher who ever lived. He taught the same way, but he called them parables."

Dan's previous writing efforts have resulted in Church productions and local publications as well as three previous best-selling novels in the Angels series: *Angels Don't Knock, Just Call Me an Angel,* and *Angels to the Rescue.*

A former bishop and high councilman, Dan and his wife, Shelby Jean, live in Phoenix, Arizona. They have six children and eighteen grandchildren. He loves to hear from his readers, who can write to him at yates@swlink.net.